JOEY MARSILIO

Henry Garrison:

St. Dante's Savior

ISBN: 0988181606
ISBN-13: 978-0-9881816-0-1

Chapter One

As Henry Garrison ran laps for his P.E. class one gray October morning, he became faintly aware of the smell of urine. His zombie-like state was shattered by a growing horror as he began to piece together just where the odor was emanating from.

Flashback to two weeks prior: Doug Seville, who had a locker next to Henry's, leaned over as they changed into their P.E. uniforms and said, "I'm gonna show that guy, the one that refuses to use a lock."

Every locker in the locker room had a padlock on it except for a single one near Doug's. The P.E. uniform inside the locker had a name written on it in black sharpie, but said name was so minuscule and faded that no one was quite sure whose it was. Henry and Doug would often joke that whoever used the locker was awfully arrogant to not be using a lock, and that they should be taught a lesson, but as far as Henry was concerned, it was all talk.

Doug, to his dubious credit, was more of an action man, and so on this particular day, he announced to Henry that he was going for it.

"What are you going to do?" said Henry.

"It's hubris, is what it is," said Doug, ignoring the question. "This is really for the guy's own good. He needs to learn that he's not above us all."

"I don't know, man," said Henry, but Doug had already snatched the uniform out of the unlocked locker and was heading toward the bathroom. He was back in a matter of moments, empty-handed.

"Where'd you put it?"

"I threw it into the bathroom stall," said Doug, rubbing his hands as if dusting them off.

"Like into the toilet?"

"I don't know. I didn't look. I just threw it over the top of the stall."

Henry and Doug had both had a laugh about the situation, then headed to class and promptly forgot about it. It had been forgotten so completely, in fact, that when Henry had come in on this particular morning and found his locker (which he had forgotten to padlock) broken into and his uniform stolen, he was thankful to find the perpetually unlocked locker to be both open and containing a uniform. One's just as good as another, Henry figured, and I'm not about to get points deducted from my grade for being out of uniform. He quickly changed into the foreign clothes and jogged out to class.

As the stale reek of urine caused these memories to come flooding into Henry's hazy mind, his stomach shuddered. These clothes obviously had landed in the toilet when Doug heaved them into the stall. God knows what else had been in there when they landed, or what happened to them in between that and their return to the locker. In fact, how had they gotten back into the locker, anyway? Whose clothes were these?

"Jeez, dude," said Doug, jogging next to him, "what's that smell? Did you have an accident or something?"

"Do you remember when you threw that guy's uniform into the toilet a couple weeks ago?" Henry said, his throat tightening.

"Oh, yeah," Doug said, laughing. "What a moron."

"Well, I'm wearing that moron's uniform. And I don't think he's washed it since."

Doug exploded with laughter, prompting a glare from Coach Grisham, who pivoted slightly in his folding chair. His already uncomfortably short nylon shorts hiked up a bit.

"Temper that enthusiasm," Coach Grisham said. Then he took a swig from his Thermos and coughed into his closed fist.

"Dude, that is insane," said Doug. "Why the hell would you put that on? You smell like a septic tank."

"I forgot!" said Henry. "I didn't know it actually went *into* the toilet. Anyway, I would've figured whoever owns it would've washed it by now. Certainly before putting it back in the locker, anyway."

"Yeah, who is this person? Why would they put it back in there and leave it for weeks without washing it? Have they been wearing it this whole time?"

"I don't know, man," Henry said, unable to resist the sick urge to sniff his pungent shirt, "but I'm wearing it right now. Unfortunately."

It was the single longest class Henry had ever suffered through. Every second dragged by as if weighed down by some intensely shameful anchor. He performed even more terribly than usual at his every athletic effort; the ordinary frivolity of pickleball was overshadowed by the incessant thoughts of being covered in someone else's urine. If it was *just* urine. Besides that fact, the class ended up running several minutes past the end-of-period bell, prolonging Henry's unhygienic agony.

"This sucks," Henry said to Doug as they hustled into the locker room. "I don't even have time to shower before the next class."

"Just do it. Be late," said Doug. "Who cares?"

"My econ teacher," said Henry, stripping off the foul garments. "She told me if I was late one more time, she'd have to talk to my parents about my perpetual tardiness."

"So you'd rather soak in filth all day than get in trouble?"

"More or less," said Henry. He stuffed the uniform into the unlocked locker and slammed it shut. "My parents have enough to deal with right now. They'll kill me if I get in any more trouble.

Literally kill me. Like, intestines draped across the living room."

"Well then," said Doug with a grin, "have a wonderful day. Hey, maybe you should rub a lemon all over yourself so you can smell like a urinal cake."

Economics class proceeded at a similarly plodding pace to P.E. Though comforted by the fact that he had his own, relatively clean clothes on again, Henry could not rid himself of the grim thought that he was coated in a thin film of stale urine. He stayed wide-eyed and well-postured so that Ms. Tegg's watchful eye would perceive him as attentive, but his disgust prevented him from focusing to any useful degree.

Midway through the class, Denise Hargrove, with her shiny hair and amber eyes, looked over at Henry and whispered, "You smell weird."

Henry's cheeks heated like embers of humiliation. He looked down at his desk and said, "Yeah. I know."

"Why? What is it?" said Denise, squinting.

"I'd really rather not get into it," said Henry. He was starting to feel a tightness in his head, like his mind was swelling to a size too large for his brain to contain.

"Well, you really smell," said Denise.

"Thanks."

"So wait, it's not even your own pee? It's someone else's?" said Trent Abner at lunch time. Trent was a part of Henry's usual group of friends that always hung out during lunch. Doug Seville was another, as was Albert Li. They congregated in the walkway in front of wood shop, which was an elevated position that separated them from the rest of the kids but allowed them to observe most of the campus. Trent was a gangly fellow with perpetual raccoon eyes and a sandpaper laugh. All of his clothes looked like they had been washed about a million times and run through a dryer full of granite. But at least they were clean.

"Yeah, no. Lord knows whose it is," Henry lamented.

"Probably Coach Grisham's," said Doug. "I heard his thermos is full of vodka. He probably has to pee like twenty times a day."

"Who told you that?" said Albert. Albert was a short guy

who always seemed to be pondering something unknown to the world. He was the quietest of Henry's group, though that really wasn't saying very much.

"I know his T.A.," said Doug. "Honestly, he swears Grisham goes into the bathroom to puke during class at least a couple of times a week. Hey, maybe you got some of that on you too, Henry."

"Great," said Henry, taking a bite of his turkey sandwich. "This is disgusting. I hate how these sandwiches get all smashed and warm in my backpack. I don't even want to eat them half of the time."

"Just think about the excrement that's probably rubbing off your hands onto the bread. That'll get your appetite up," Trent said through a mouthful of french fries. Some errant ketchup had left a burgundy glob on his shirt, but on this day there was no way he could be labeled the untidy one.

"I washed my hands, dumbass," said Henry, who stopped chewing and wrinkled his nose. "It's the rest that's a problem."

"You should get a lunchbox," said Albert. "That'll keep your sandwich from being smashed."

"Huh," said Henry. "You know, you may be onto something there. Maybe if I got like a Batman lunchbox or something. Maybe that'd be cool."

"Nobody carries a lunch box anymore," said Doug. "This isn't third grade. You'll look like a *tool*box if you carry one around. Even a Batman one."

"Whatever," said Henry. "I don't need to be like everybody else. I can't stand everybody else. Besides, I'm sick of these smashed sandwiches."

"I'm sick of your mom," said Doug.

"She's sick of you," said Henry. "And I'm totally getting a lunchbox."

"You should get a *Ghostbusters* one," said Albert.

"*My Little Pony*," said Trent.

As soon as Henry got home, he practically sprinted upstairs to the shower, dodging his parents as they unpacked cardboard boxes in the living room. As he ascended the creaky staircase with a much faster pace than he could ever muster in P.E., his mom called up to him, "Hi Henry! How was your day?"

"Disgusting," said Henry as he fled into the bathroom, closed the door, and practically leaped into the shower.

Post-shower, Henry descended the stairs in some fresh clothing. Drips of water ran from his wet hair down the back of his neck like insects, but the sensation was strangely comforting coming off today's horror. The aroma of soap that emanated from his moist skin had never been so wonderful. Henry was high on hygiene.

"What do you mean, your day was disgusting?" said Henry's mother, who had moved into the kitchen and begun to prepare dinner while Henry was bathing. "What happened?"

"Well, my clothes definitely need to be washed. Maybe burned," Henry sighed. "But it's over with, and I really don't want to dwell on it anymore than I already have. Oh, and I'm going to have to buy a new P.E. uniform tomorrow. Somebody stole mine."

"What? How could that happen?" said his mother.

"I forgot to lock my locker. I'm sorry. Believe me, I've been amply punished for this."

"Henry, you really have to be more careful about these

things. You know we can't afford to just be-"

"It's OK," said Henry. "I'll pay for it. Don't worry. It's my fault. I don't expect you to have to deal with it."

"No, no. I don't want you to have to pay for it," said his mother. "It's just...we can't be wasting money on things like this."

"I know, I know. I'm sorry," said Henry. "Like I said, I'll pay for it. Don't even think about it."

"Just...please be more careful," said his mother. As she stirred a pot at the stove, Henry's father walked in the kitchen.

"Hey, dad," Henry said, "how's it going?"

"It's...going," said his father, shaking his head slightly. "Back hurts from unpacking these boxes. No calls for a job. You know. The usual." He shuffled back into the living room. Henry's father had never been the most chipper man, but ever since he was laid off from his job as a computer salesman a few months ago, his mood had steadily decayed to a perpetual dour malaise.

"How's your room going?" Henry's mom asked. "Is everything unpacked yet?"

"Getting there," said Henry. "Where's Grandma?"

"She's asleep," his mother said. "She hasn't been feeling well lately. She's probably just tired, what with everything going on."

"Yeah, I guess," said Henry. "Alright, well, let me know when dinner's ready."

Henry went upstairs to his room and closed the door, then sat on his bed and looked around. He still wasn't used to this room; honestly, he wasn't even used to this house. It was just so *old*...not that their old house had been the Bellagio or anything, but this place was like the Haunted Mansion's guest cottage. Everything was dusty and ancient, and each room had these small, wooden-shuttered windows that let light enter through narrow slits, like horizontal prison bars. However, it was paid for, and had been for some time. That was the important part, and the fatal flaw of their old place. It was probably for the best. His grandmother had clearly been lonesome for a while, and Henry could hardly blame her for that; how could anyone stand to live in a house by this all by themselves? And he did have a much bigger closet here than at the old place. It was still creepy, though.

Henry stood up and was briefly jolted by the sight of his reflection in the mirror popping into his peripheral vision. Taking a deep breath, he squatted next to one of the few boxes left unpacked and opened up the flaps. He immediately smiled. Among the box's contents was the Nintendo Entertainment System he had bought at a flea market shortly before the move. He had found it among an assortment of random knickknacks presided over by a swarthy man who spoke approximately seven and a half words of English, two of which happened to be "ten dollars." Between this, and a handful of games he had picked up for nearly nothing from an extremely bored-looking housewife with very large platinum blonde hair, he had purchased the finest entertainment 1985 had to offer for less than $20. He hadn't gotten to play it much before he packed it, but it was his once again. Deciding to neglect both unpacking and homework for the time being, he plugged the system into his television, put in *Super Mario Bros.*, and prepared to be blown away.

Except the power light refused to illuminate, remaining a mocking black square. Henry pressed and repressed the power and reset buttons. Nothing. He unplugged the system and inserted the

AC adapter into a different wall socket. Nothing. He checked all the connections. Nothing. He pounded on it with a few square shots with his fists. The same. It must have gotten damaged during the move. The king was dead.

Mumbling obscenities, Henry went back to his bed. He picked up his iPod from the nightstand, put on his headphones, and started listening to the nastiest, most profane music he could think of. Then he pulled his history textbook out of his backpack and cracked it open to Chapter 13. As he began to read about the Industrial Revolution, he could have sworn he still smelled urine, faintly.

Chapter Two

St. Dante, California had been Henry's home for his entire life. A small town 30 miles east of San Jose, it was a pleasant enough community, framed by the woods that ran along the southern and eastern borders and the hills to the north. There was exactly one public school at each educational level; currently, Henry was attending the rather blandly monikered St. Dante High School. The local prison was minuscule, and crime was limited mostly to youthful mischief, with anything more serious serving as a shocking aberration. It was the sort of community where, fifty years ago, everyone would have known one another; nowadays, people spent too much time on their couches to get a sense of the community at large. Nonetheless, there was an air of insular familiarity to St. Dante that didn't exist in larger cities. Whether or not that was a good thing depended entirely upon who you asked.

Though the uneventful atmosphere of St. Dante at times

drove Henry up the wall, he took a certain comfort in knowing that there was not an excessive number of people he would have to leapfrog in order to be St. Dante's greatest success story. How exactly this leapfrogging was supposed to occur, Henry was unsure, but he assumed he'd figure it out sooner or later.

The downside to small town living, however, was abundantly evident this particular Saturday. All of Henry's friends were otherwise occupied, his parents were hardly the most exciting type-they never met reality television they didn't like-and his stupid Nintendo was broken. His eyes burning from staring at his computer monitor, Henry realized he couldn't spend his entire day online and decided to see if his grandmother has any ideas for him.

"I don't know," his grandmother said. "Look at me. I never do anything, except go to the store, and why would you want to go to the store? Unless you do. But I don't think you do, or else you would have just gone already."

"Yeah, I don't want to go to the store," said Henry.

"Well, if you're really bored, you can go dig around in the attic. Bunch of crap up there, but you might find something you want."

"What kind of stuff is up there?"

"Crap. Junk. Mostly. I don't know, I can't be bothered. I haven't even been up there in I don't know how long, so who knows. But there are old records and stuff. Things you haven't seen before, I'm sure."

After listening to his grandmother talk about syndicated judge shows and minorities for a while, Henry went back to his room and, after a lengthy period of nothing, decided to check out the attic. He put on an old black Metallica t-shirt in anticipation of epidemic levels of dust, and headed up the creaky ladder into the attic's trapdoor. He was fairly impressed by what he saw.

There was nothing that stood out as hugely interesting, but there was quite a bit to sort through. Piles of old boxes littered the spacious attic. Pale light from the single small window shown upon a rocking horse that had lost one of its opaque glass eyes. Further, there were stacks of magazines with flaky, yellow pages and antiquated articles about New Zealand and keeping one's kitchen spotless. An old weight set weighing down a flimsy, warped set of shelves. Beatles dolls that were probably worth some money, even in their less than optimal condition.

Henry leafed through a pile of magazines, small jaundiced bits of paper free-falling to the floor. He found a single old *Playboy*, and was interested for a moment until realizing that a) the woman he was ogling was very, very old if not dead by now, and b) it was way tamer than the stuff he looked at online all the time. Moving right along, he saw some *National Geographic*s and *Good Housekeeping*s and decided that he was bored with the magazine portion of his investigation. Moving on…

He sorted through several unmarked boxes, and found some old Coca-Cola bottles, buttons, strange toys (including a pair of hideous marionettes with elongated, emaciated bodies and the faces of a mournful jester and grinning Satan, respectively) and tools. His eyes were starting to water and burn from the sheer amount of dust, and he started to wish he was equipped with one of those white medical face masks. Looking to flee the airborne particles, Henry looked around for anything else that might be of immediate interest before he gave his sinuses some respite. In this final sweep of the attic, he noticed a small cabinet in the very back, mostly concealed by a clothes rack and several stained cardboard boxes. Amidst the clutter, the sight of something hidden piqued Henry's curiosity. He shoved the clothes and boxes out of the way and yanked on the cabinet's door, but it seemed to be locked. Henry ran his hand over the rough wood and noted a lack of a lock anywhere; what exactly was holding this door closed was not immediately apparent. Undeterred, he grabbed the tarnished brass handle and pulled with all of his might. He felt a little bit of give and pulled again. The handle cut into the flesh of his palm, and a bit of blood oozed onto the handle. Annoyed, Henry gave one final tug of frustration. He fell backwards as the door ripped completely out, the hinges still clinging to jagged shards of wood that sat suspended in midair. He inhaled deeply in shock, filling his lungs with dust like a vacuum bag.

Henry hacked sharply, and wheezed as tears welled up in the corners of his eyes. He let out a hoarse, haggard groan as he practically sneezed his soul out. Leaving a crimson hand print as he pushed himself up, Henry rose from the dusty floor, and regulated his breathing. He widened his eyes and blinked a few times, then wiped his soggy eyeballs as he shook his head. Glancing at the cabinet door that had broken off in his fist, he looked around for a place to stash it in order to avoid a lecture on property destruction. Eventually he decided to just cover the gaping cabinet opening with some of the attic's abundant cardboard boxes and hope no one noticed for the foreseeable future; after all, who else was going to be poking around up here?

As Henry shoved the stained boxes back up against the opening, he leaned over and looked inside to see whether the secrets that lie within had been worth his bloody palm and shredded lungs. His curiosity was rewarded, as shrouded in the darkness of the unsealed cabinet was a wooden box. It looked handmade; it was warped and uneven, with a dull finish and visibly oxidized nail heads on the sides. A single crack ran down the middle of the box, but despite its flaws, it seemed sturdy. Henry snatched the box and tucked it under his arm, then shoved the other boxes and clothes back into place to cover up his mishap. Still sniffling, he descended the attic ladder into the rest of the house, and shut the trapdoor.

Henry went into his room and caught a glimpse of himself in the mirror. His eyes were a stoner-esque red, and his hair was webbed with gobs of gray dust. He had mucus dried and caked above his upper lip, and his shirt was smeared with the filth of attic antiquity. Crudely made as the wooden box was, it was probably the most attractive aspect of him at that point. He grimaced and sat down on the floor, holding the box in his lap. Holding it up, he rotated it as he tried to figure out how it opened; apparently, the box was nailed shut. This was becoming far too much work.

A few minutes and a couple more scratches later, Henry was back in his room with a claw hammer, working the nails out of the box with an annoyed determination. The scent of cedar wafted up to his dust-clogged nostrils as the wood split and surrendered before the claw. Finally, the final nail slid out of the wood, and the final splinter wedged itself within Henry's epidermis. Henry removed the lid and stared within the box, more out of a sense of duty than excitement. And sure enough, there was nothing all that exciting within.

A black ball of worn, sunbleached leather lay at the top of the box. Henry removed it and found that the ball was actually an old pair of gloves wrapped around something else. As he unwound the gloves from one another, a heavy metal cylinder fell out onto the carpet. It definitely was the most striking item amidst the contents of the box; it was composed of a bright, rich yellow metal that was unlike any Henry had ever seen. It seemed to be made of several interlocking pieces; one of them, in the center of the object, was a dull emerald green. It weighed more than its appearance belied, and had a perplexing anachronistic quality to it, especially compared to those tattered leather gloves. Beneath that, there was a tattered, leather-bound book; there was no writing on the cover, though it seemed to be a journal of some sort. It was in better shape than the gloves, at least.

As Henry held up the metal cylinder and huffed at its surprising mass, his cell phone rang. He put the cylinder back in the box with the gloves and journal, and picked up his phone just as the second iteration of the theme from *Ghostbusters* that he had selected as his ringtone on a whim was nearly finished playing.

"Yello'," said Henry.

"Hey man," said Doug on the other end. "We're going to get some dinner. Do you want to come with us?"

"Who is 'us?'" Henry said, picking at a splinter in his palm.

"Me and some people," said Doug.

"How descriptive."

"We're leaving in fifteen. Are you coming?"

"Yeah, I'll go. I need to take a shower and stuff, though."

"Well, hurry up. We'll be there in a half hour."

"Who is 'we?'" Henry said.

"Us. See you then," said Doug, who then hung up.

Henry glanced at himself in the mirror once more. There was no way the person or persons accompanying Doug were as exciting as his vagueness implied, but just in case, Henry had to at least attempt to not look horrendous. He dashed into the bathroom, his mental timer ticking away, the wooden box and its contents abandoned near the foot of his bed.

"So this is the lunchbox I eventually decided on," said

Henry, lifting up his neon-green acquisition for his friends' perusal as they walked to their respective first classes. It was emblazoned with the scowling images of Lebanese pop duo L.E.B.S. They were an attractive pair of diminutive black-haired pixies that made out with each other on stage and wrote songs about lipstick and totalitarianism. "I think it's pretty awesome, personally."

"L.E.B.S., huh?" said Trent. "What, they didn't have any ones with rainbows and unicorns on them?"

"Oh, they did," said Henry. "But come on, two hot Lebanese chicks on a lunchbox. What's wrong with that?"

"Where to begin…" said Trent.

"Well, they *are* lesbians," said Albert. "That's cool, right?"

"Faux lesbians," said Henry. "One of them has kids. Maybe both of them. They're contract lesbians, I think."

"You certainly seem to know a lot about them. When are their birthdays?" said Trent.

"I don't know. But what can I say? I like them. They have good songs."

"I guess," said Trent. "If you're into that sort of thing."

"I am," said Henry, who separated from the pack. "See you guys later."

Henry walked towards his P.E. class with a slight grin, proud of his lunchbox while still cognizant of its absurdity. As he swung it by his side with perhaps a bit too much zeal, he became conscious of a chuckle behind him. Henry whirled around to stare in the green eyes of Roderick King III, half closed in the scrunch that tends to accompany derisive laughter. Roderick was the son of Richard King, St. Dante's resident super-entrepreneur and head of King Industries, a multifaceted corporation with a local company headquarters and an unmistakably cheesy crown logo. Because of this, Roderick was obscenely wealthy and carried with him a sense of entitlement the size of an arrogance-fueled zeppelin. He was flanked by a couple of faithful flunkies Henry recognized by sight, but whose names he had never bothered to learn. They wore a matching pair of smirks.

"Something funny, Rod?" Henry asked as he came to a stop. "Don't leave me out of the joke."

"You *are* the joke, Garrison," Roderick said, grinning. His teeth were annoyingly white. "That's an adorable lunchbox you've got there. Did your mommy pick it up for you at Wal-Mart?"

"No," said Henry. "I bought it myself." He immediately winced at the realization of how ineffectual this retort was.

"Well good job," said Roderick as his cronies sneered. "Maybe she'll let you start dressing yourself soon, too! Why the hell do you need a lunchbox, anyway? So you have a place to put your Fruit Roll-Ups and Yoo-Hoo?"

"...No," said Henry. He gazed at the ground. "I don't have time for this, Roderick. I've got to get to class."

"Toodles," said Roderick. As Henry continued his journey to class, head down, Roderick and his friends passed a chuckle between them like a can of nitrous oxide.

"What a jerk," said Henry a couple of hours later as he took a chug from his bottle of Yoo-Hoo. He and his friends were sitting in their usual lunchtime spot. As he tore off a piece of his Fruit Roll-Up, he groused, "Making fun of my lunchbox. Where does he get off?"

"You kind of set yourself up for it by, you know, carrying a

L.E.B.S. lunchbox," said Doug. He took a bite of apple and wiped a dribble of juice off his chin. "Though I'll agree that he is, in fact, a jerk."

"I don't get it," said Henry, chewing angrily. "It's a lunchbox. It's funny. Who cares? I mean, in my econ class, Denise Hargrove told me how stupid it was. Out of the blue. Is it really that bad?"

"Hey, your sandwich isn't crushed, right?" Trent said. Like clockwork, he once again had ketchup on his shirt from his french fries. But then, he wasn't the one carrying a lunchbox.

"No, it's actually really nice today," said Henry, looking down at the sandwich for no real reason.

"Well, then, there you go," said Trent.

"Yeah, if you really want to be embarrassed about something, you should be embarrassed about how you played in the softball game this morning. Damn," said Doug.

"Oh, shut up," said Henry. "My hands are all cut up and full of splinters. I can barely grip the bat. Besides, I'm tired. If I had known we were gonna be out so late last night, I wouldn't have gone."

"Yes you would have," Doug said. "Hanging out and being bored is much more fun in a group than it is individually."

"I guess."

"So are you guys going to the Halloween dance?" said Albert. He looked around at everyone's faces, blinking.

Trent laughed. "You've got to be kidding," he said. "When have any of us ever gone to a dance?"

"Hey, I go sometimes," said Doug.

"Yeah, yeah. You don't count," said Trent. "Why would you even ask that question, dude?"

"Well, I mean, I think I'm going, and I just wanted to know if it's just gonna be me or if one of you is coming," said Albert.

"Wait, hold on," said Trent. "*You're* going? You? You've never gone to a dance, have you?"

"No," said Albert. "But I asked Jenny to go, and..."

"Jenny Carlson?" said Trent. "My ass. Are you serious?"

"She's cute," said Doug. "In the sort of like, librarian field mouse way. I'd hit it."

"Thanks," said Albert slowly. "Uh, yeah, she wants to go with me, I guess. I mean, I asked her, and she said OK, so I figure she wants to go, right?"

"Unbelievable," said Trent. "I can't picture you ever asking a girl out. Why would you do that?"

"Because I like her. Duh," said Albert. Tiny beads of sweat were forming on his forehead.

"Well, hey, good for you," said Trent. "I just can't picture it, is all. But congratulations. I'm still not going to the dance, but I'm happy for you."

"What about you, Henry?" said Albert.

"I don't think so," Henry said. He gestured to the throng of students in the main quad. "I get enough of these people as it is without having to spend my Friday night with them too. But nice job on the Jenny thing. Really."

"Why don't you ask Denise Hargrove?" Doug said. "I'm sure between the pee smell and the lunchbox, she's just sitting by the phone waiting for your call."

"You're as much of a jerk as Roderick, dude," said Henry,

guzzling the last of his Yoo-Hoo. "Maybe worse."

"Yeah," said Trent. "But Roderick dresses better."

"Shut up, dude," said Doug. "I like this shirt."

That night, Henry had an unusually immense amount of homework, and just barely finished up by 11 o' clock. He went to sleep almost immediately afterwards, and had a very strange dream. In it, he was walking somewhere in the mountains, and everything had a deep purple tint. He was all alone, as far as he could tell, surrounded by bushy outcroppings of thick grass and weathered gray stones. He wandered aimlessly, and found a cave that for some reason he could not enter. He stood before it and gazed in, and as he did, two large red eyes glared back at him from the darkness. Henry stood, frozen, and the eyes just stared and stared. They did not move, nor did they blink, nor did the figure who possessed the eyes ever step forward. They just fixed coldly upon Henry's eyes, a pair of will-o'-the-wisps with a chokehold on his soul. The standoff finally ended as Henry's alarm went off and he groaned and rolled over, soaked in sweat. He clicked the alarm off and sighed; the eyes still burned in his brain. He tried to shake off a lingering case of the creeps and threw off his comforter, only to find his room distressingly cold. Leaping up, he rushed over to his closet to find some warmer clothes, pausing briefly to check the mirror for any pairs of menacing red eyes.

After he had brushed his teeth and otherwise prepared himself for the day, Henry threw on a black, zip-up hooded sweatshirt and his backpack. He was rubbing his hands together, dreading the frigid morning air he was about to plunge into, when it occurred to him that he had just come into possession of a pair of gloves that, worn or not, would be far warmer than bare hands. He rummaged them out of the box and, clutching them, went downstairs. He grabbed his lunchbox from his mother, thanked her for preparing his lunch, and said goodbye as he stepped out the front door. Wedging the lunchbox in his left armpit, Henry slipped on the pair of gloves. They were a pretty good fit, and very comfortable. As he flexed his fingers inside them, he felt a strange sensation run through his body. It was a very pleasant warmth, a sort of tingle that made him feel lighter than air. It coursed through him, head to toe, energizing his very being. Looking at the gloves in wonder, Henry shrugged it off; he felt the best he had in a long time, so whatever the reason, he wasn't going to worry about it. He headed off down the street, unable to keep from smiling. He felt like he was practically floating.

Upon reaching St. Dante High, Henry didn't see anyone around he particularly cared to talk to, so he just walked straight to P.E. class. When he reached the heavy orange door that marked the boys' locker room, Henry firmly grasped the knob, turned it, and pulled.

The door ripped off the hinges in his hand like a piece of cotton candy. The entire locker room turned and stared, gape mouthed, as Henry held the door aloft as though it were made of tissue paper. His hand still wrapped around the doorknob, he effortlessly moved the entire door up and down.

"Holy crap," he said.

Chapter Three

"Look, I'm sure you think this is real funny," said Mr. Sadek, the principal of St. Dante High School, as he leaned over his cluttered desk. "But don't expect the school to have to pay for your vandalism."

"Hey, I'm sorry," said Henry. He was squirming in an uncomfortable brown plastic chair that was as least as old as he was. "I didn't do it on purpose. I don't even know how it happened!"

"Really," said Mr. Sadek. "Well, doors don't just come off, Henry. They don't just leap off their hinges like ballerinas."

"Huh? Ballerinas?" said Henry.

"I'm not stupid," said Mr. Sadek, easing himself back into his seat and gripping his mug of lukewarm coffee. "I know you must have tampered with that door. I'm sure you just wanted to be *cool.* Wanted some attention. Well if it's attention you want, Henry, you've got mine. Undivided. And it's not a good thing for you."

"I swear, I'm not looking for attention," said Henry. His hands were clasped uncomfortably in his lap; he couldn't really figure out what to do with them. His gloves were balled up in his pocket, and his clammy hands were the polar opposite of warmth and comfort at the moment. "I don't know what happened. Maybe somebody else messed with the door and I just happened to be the one who pulled it off."

"Hmm," said Mr. Sadek. "Well, the hinges are destroyed, so it's going to be a costly ordeal getting it back on. I hope your parents don't mind paying for it."

"Oh, please, don't make them," said Henry. "I'll accept whatever punishment, I don't care. Just please don't make my parents pay for anything. They're going through some really hard times, and I can't...I can't do this to them."

Mr. Sadek tilted his head to one side and exhaled sharply. "One month of detention," he said. "Don't let this happen again."

"Fine. Thank you. I won't," Henry said, nodding his head apologetically.

Walking out of the principal's office, Henry glanced at his

watch, a cheap rubber rust-colored digital deal he had picked up for seven dollars. He had missed most of P.E. class, so there was really no sense in going back for the last few minutes; by the time he changed and got out there, class would probably be over. Besides, he had a few more pressing things on his mind. What exactly had happened this morning? Why had the door come off? Yes, maybe someone had tampered with it, but even so, why had he been able to pick up the broken door single-handed, like it was nothing?

To his left, Henry spotted a fairly large, smooth black stone near the bushes, and he walked over and picked it up. The stone was no lighter than he expected; actually, it was a bit heavier. Perplexed, he tossed the stone back down. It left his hands with a residual chill, which combined with the frosty, misty air to make his palms and knuckles ache with cold. He fished around for the gloves in his sweatshirt pocket and put them on. Instantly, he once again felt the warm, light tingle he had experienced this morning. Newly comforted, a thought popped into his head. A peculiar, ridiculous thought, of course...but what could be the harm in testing it out? He slowly leaned over and placed his hand upon the black stone, whose coldness he could no longer feel with the gloves on.

He jerked the rock up, towards him. It felt weightless, nearly nonexistent. Henry's heart pounded in his chest as he lightly rubbed the stone. It was as though the stone was suddenly made out of styrofoam. As his stomach gurgled, Henry squeezed the stone. A deep fissure formed in the middle at his squeeze; one of the newly formed halves fell to the ground with a clack that echoed across the temporarily empty hallway. His eyes wide, Henry squeezed the remaining half and it crumbled like sand. He let the stone's remains spill out from between his fingers, slowly accumulating into a pile of dust as he stood in place, quaking. This couldn't possibly be happening...and yet, it was.

Henry looked around to see if anyone was watching him. Not seeing anyone, he hastily took the gloves off and put them back in his pocket. He slowed his breathing rate and tried to calm himself, perspiring despite the cold. Vibrating with excitement and fear, the blare of the period bell spurred him into motion, and he headed to his next class. On his way there, he passed hundreds of students, but didn't notice a single one.

It was one of the strangest school days Henry had ever experienced. He did not pay attention to anything any of his teachers said, and only noticed when class was over because everyone else started getting up. He felt faint, and extremely impatient. At lunch time, he had to answer to his friends regarding the morning's incident; word had traveled pretty quickly about Henry dismantling the locker room door. Playing it off as a weird coincidence, Henry had very little to say, letting his friends go on at length about it while he nervously fondled the gloves in his pocket. He was tempted, so tempted, to put them on to perform some radical feat of strength in front of everyone. But he didn't know whether or not it would work again, and even if it did, what exactly would he do? He decided to leave these questions unanswered for the moment and experiment with the gloves later. For the time being, he munched away on his cool, unsquashed sandwich and chuckled when appropriate.

Detention was equally agonizing, with Henry counting the minutes while trying to figure out how exactly he was going to explain this incident to his parents. Still, when his thoughts returned to the gloves, he couldn't help but grin.

When school let out, Henry decided not to go home immediately, instead opting to head into the woods by himself. He walked to a clearing that, on warm days, often played host to a smattering of teenagers laying around, chattering and gesticulating and possibly smoking something ostensibly medicinal. Today, though, there was no one around but Henry. A thick, serpentine mist wound through the trees, having never dissipated from this morning. Taking a long look around to make sure that he was alone, Henry slipped the gloves on. The chill of the woods melted away as the tingle which was rapidly becoming familiar radiated through his being. His hands balled into fists, he looked up at the swirling autumn sky. Time to see what he could do.

The first test was a simple one: how hard could he hit something? He walked up to a sizable tree and scratched the back of his neck. Based on what he had done to the stone earlier, he had every reason to believe he could punch through the tree. But it sounded like an immensely painful thing to do; he wasn't one of those martial artists that could shatter concrete with their hands. He didn't have any training, and regardless of his strength, he figured that trying to put his fist through a tree was sure to leave him with some bone and tissue damage. Then again, how was he to know his limits if he refused to test himself? With a snort, Henry decided to take a "nothing ventured, nothing gained" approach, and drew back his fist. He threw a punch and…stopped short. He couldn't go through with it. Not on his first attempt, nor his second, nor his third. Finally, accepting pain as inevitable, he closed his eyes and thrust his fist forward with all the force he could muster.

When he opened his eyes, he found no pain, nor any damage to his fist or even his glove. He did find, however, a massive hole through the tree that his arm happened to be mostly within. Breathless in his excitement, he drew his hand out and shook off the loose bits of bark and pulp. This was beyond surreal.

Deciding that busting holes in trees was not the most environmentally friendly way of demonstrating his newfound might, Henry looked for different avenues. He crushed a few rocks in his hands and kicked a pinecone who knows how far. He then had an unfortunate mental image of it landing on an unsuspecting kitten, and subsequently hoped for the pinecone to follow a safe, uneventful path. He managed to punch shoulder-deep into the Earth with minimal effort. At this point, Henry began to wonder if perhaps he might have some other sort of power he wasn't aware of; after all, Superman was strong, but he could fly and was invincible and so on and so forth. Sure, it was far-fetched, but then, so was everything else about the current situation. So he decided to try to fly. Having never flown before, however, he had no idea how one might do such a thing. What muscles was he supposed to flex? After a few minutes of straining and clenching that he was glad would never be witnessed by anyone, Henry decided to give up on the flying thing and try something a bit less abstract. To see if the gloves had increased his speed, he decided to dash into the woods...and promptly moved so quickly that he smashed right into an oak tree. Thankfully, much like his tree punching, the collision didn't actually hurt; it was more exhilarating than anything.

As Henry pushed himself up from the ground, he realized that it had started to drizzle. Yet he couldn't feel the rain. It ran off of him in tiny streams, but didn't seem to make any contact with his skin. Regardless, it seemed like a good time to head back home; his parents would be wondering where he was, and he didn't really have any other ideas for how to use his power just yet. As he turned to go home (not full speed; he didn't need to be bashing into things all the way home), he had one last idea: perhaps he couldn't fly, but how high could he jump? Before thinking it through, he leaped into the air and found himself soaring well above the treetops, ending up about seventy feet in the air. Which was all well and good, except for the grim realization that he was going to have to land, and it was going to hurt. His teeth gritted, his eyes slammed shut in prayer, Henry landed in the muddying dirt, crouching, with a light thud, but no discomfort. Opening his right eye slowly, he patted himself down to find everything in its proper place. He fell on his backside as his astonishment gave way to elation, and Henry just laughed and laughed.

"Where have you been?" Henry's mother asked him as he stepped into the house. She was in the kitchen with Henry's grandmother, making dinner. Henry's father was sitting on the couch, reading the newspaper. He looked up at Henry and grunted, then went back to the paper.

"I've, uh, well," said Henry. He wrestled with his conscience for a moment before saying, "I got in trouble at school, so I had detention. I'm actually going to have it for a month."

"What?" said Henry's father. "That's ridiculous. A month?"

"Yeah," said Henry. "But it's not so bad."

"Not so bad?" said Henry's mother, stepping out into the living room. "It must have been pretty bad...they don't just hand out a *month* of detention for nothing."

"No, I know. I ripped a door off the hinges," said Henry.

"Ripped a door off the hinges?" said Henry's father.

"Yeah, no, hear me out," said Henry. "I can explain the whole thing. Well, I think I can, sort of. And it's good news for us. Really."

"How is your getting into trouble good news for us?" said Henry's mother. "With everything else going on, I don't..."

Henry wanted to tell his family about everything. The truth

was turning a crank in his head, forcing his mouth open and pushing the words out. But he caught himself, and held back. He wasn't sure he was ready to tell anyone about this. Not yet, not until he had some idea what was happening to him and what he wanted to do with it. This could be the hope that his family so badly needed...however, once they found out, Henry knew things would never be the same. And he was not prepared for that.

"You're right," he said. "I'm sorry. I don't know what I was thinking. It was just...it was just stupid. But the good part is, we won't have to pay for the repairs. So that's not bad."

Sighing, Henry's mother went back into the kitchen.

"Well, I guess it would be pointless to ground you," said Henry's father with his eyebrow raised, "seeing as how the school sort of did that anyway."

"But I'm guessing you're still pretty mad," said Henry.

His father shrugged. "Meh," he said. "You didn't kill anyone."

And that seemed to be that. Henry's father was back to the

newspaper as if nothing had happened, and his mom was frying something that snapped and sizzled and smelled scrumptious. She didn't look particularly pleased, but she wasn't yelling at him, so he figured he might as well just go upstairs and wait for dinner. As he turned toward the stairs, his grandmother grabbed his arm.

"So you tore a door of the hinges?" she asked.

"Yeah," said Henry. "I know. Wacky."

"Yes, but how?"

"Huh? Oh. I don't know. It was an accident, really. A freak thing."

"No. It was an accident when I fell down the stairs. You don't rip a door off by accident."

"First time for everything."

"That's what they say," she said, looking Henry in the eyes. "But what about the things that never supposed to happen? There's no first time for them. And I think this is one of those things."

"That's an interesting viewpoint," said Henry, choosing his words carefully. "But hey, life's full of surprises."

"Obviously."

As soon as he got to his room, Henry closed his door and threw his backpack to the ground. He snatched up the wooden box from beside his bed and pulled out the book and the metal cylinder. Rolling the cylinder around in his hands, he couldn't help but wonder what this peculiar object had to do with the gloves. As he ran his thumb over the cylinder's surface, he noticed that the emerald green segment was slightly raised compared to the rest of it, like a button. Wondering if perhaps it was the key to figuring out what exactly this thing was, he pressed on the segment. And screamed.

In the blink of an eye, the cylinder expanded into a nightmare. A scythe, roughly five feet long, erupted from the tiny cylinder. It was composed of the same yellowish metal, and had the same segmented look as it had before its transformation. The blade was about two feet long, and six inches wide, ending in a razor point. The tip of the shaft, near the blade, was similarly sharp, ending in a small, edged pyramid. The scythe as a whole emanated an eerie, soft blue glow that only served to make its appearance even more alien. And the very touch of it sent a wave of agony through Henry's very soul. As he dropped it to the floor, the flesh of his palm was beet red and already beginning to blister. His hand shook like he had ingested a pound of pure caffeine, and his heart felt like it might explode out of shock. Even within the context of the day's extraordinary happenings, this was just too much.

There was a knock on the door. "Henry, are you OK?" his mother called. "What happened?"

Henry looked down at the scythe, which, despite its ruinous effects on his hand, didn't seem to be damaging the floor at all. Unwilling to touch it again, but also unwilling to be discovered, he dashed over to the door and opened it just a crack.

"It's OK, mom," he said, wincing at the searing pain still radiating through his hand. "I just smashed my hand, is all. I overreacted. I'm OK."

"It sounded like you were getting slaughtered up here."

"No, no. No slaughter. Nuh-uh."

"OK," said his mother. "Do you need a band-aid or some hydrocortisone or anything?"

"I'll be fine," he said. "I'll take care of it. Thank you, though...sorry for scaring you."

"Well, I'm glad you're alright," she said. "Dinner should be ready in fifteen minutes or so."

"Great," said Henry. His hand felt like it was bathed in magma, and his voice came out much more high-pitched and strained than usual. "Thanks, mom."

"Mmm-hmm," she said. "Be careful. I don't need you in the hospital."

After she went downstairs, Henry went into the bathroom and poured some disinfectant on his hand. The additional sizzle almost made him scream again. He then put some ointment on the burn and wrapped it in gauze. It was still incredibly painful, but at least there was some sort of buffer between the wound and the outside world.

When Henry went back into his room, he stared at the scythe laying on the floor, glowing like a bug zapper. He couldn't just leave it there. What if someone found it or, God forbid, if he absent-mindedly stepped on it in his bare feet? No, he was going to have to do something with it. He thought about wrapping a towel around it, but just couldn't risk touching it again. Fishing out the gloves, he pondered whether they would be enough to prevent him from further injury. On the one hand, he couldn't think of a better way to grip the scythe; on the other hand, he didn't want to risk destroying his amazing new toys. He decided to just leave the scythe on the floor for the time being. It didn't seem to be hurting anything.

After quickly devouring his dinner and shifting nervously at the table amidst his grandmother's mealtime diatribe about getting overcharged twelve cents on bananas, Henry lay on his bed and thumbed through the leather bound book that had been within the wooden box. As he had suspected, it was in fact a journal, belonging to one Jeremiah Lee Garrison. The pages were brittle and faded, and some of the writing was illegibly light. However, what he could read was very informative, and accompanied by charmingly crude illustrations. The first couple dozen pages were nothing special, dealing mostly with agriculture, weather patterns, and anecdotes about people long-dead. But then the journal took an unexpected turn. On page 28, there was a particularly interesting entry:

August 18, 1888

I cannot say that I know how to explain what has happened today. Perhaps at some point, I will be able to look back upon it and understand. But for the time being, I remain in awe of the peculiarities I have today observed, and heartbroken at their consequences.

I had heard talk of something going on up in the hills. At first I dismissed it as idle gossip; folks around here don't seem to have enough to do, and have to make up stories to keep themselves entertained. I wish I had paid the gossip more heed...if I had, then Emily might still be alive.

For weeks, a rot had been spreading through the turnip fields. It was only this morning, though, that I inspected it more closely and realized that the blight extended far beyond the turnips; in fact, it merely seemed to end in the turnips, though it was growing by the day. There was a long trail of dead soil, brimming with rotten, wilted plants, that ran off as far as I could see, up into the hills. Figuring this as little more than a bit of bad fortune, I ignored it as best I could, and just prayed it would stop spreading soon. I had lost enough crops; I could not afford to lose many more.

Emily, I suppose, was more interested than I was in regards to where the rot was coming from. Neither I nor Beatrice saw her slip away and follow the barren trail into the hills. Apparently, Thomas saw her heading off, and followed her. God bless him for trying to take care of his little sister. I wish it had been enough.

He came to us, weeping and filthy. He was babbling; half of what he was saying was gibberish, and the other half was completely unbelievable. He was talking about a monster in the hills, saying that it had done something to Emily and would have done the same to him. He was apologizing and wailing. Beatrice cradled his head and started crying too. I didn't know what to do, but I had to do something. So I went and found my rifle and my old sword from the War, put on my leather gloves, and headed up the trail to find my daughter.

The further along the path I went, the more depleted the land got. The blight seemed to have formed a large triangle, of which my turnip field is the tip. By the time I reached the cave up in the hills, there was hardly any greenery to be seen anywhere; even the trees in the area were pale and barren. I could see some light tracks in the dirt, which indicated to me that this must be where Emily was. Gripped by fear and anger, I plunged into the darkness.

Only a few feet into the cave, I became aware of a faint glow around a bend several yards up and, wasting no time, I went to go see who might be lurking ahead. I wanted to call out to Emily, but my voice escaped me. I forced myself to slow down as I got to the lighted aperture; I didn't know who (or how many) could be in there, and I owed it to my family to exercise caution. Leaning close against the cave wall, I crept over and peered into the opening.

I have never, nor likely will ever see anything quite like what I saw in the cave. There was a small room before me, perhaps ten feet square. The walls were lined with something that looked like brass, but a much brighter yellow. Set in the brass were all manner of lamps and dials, and a few illuminated panels of some sort.

Despite this wondrous backdrop, it was hard to notice anything besides the large figure in the room. Large as a grizzly bear, it appeared to be a large man, but his attire was strange, and his flesh was gray and hairless. His back was turned to me, but I could see that he had a pair of horns atop his head-like Satan himself-but far larger, like a bull's horns. I caught a chill in his presence; though he had not yet noticed me, his very being was utterly terrifying. My terror quickly turned to nausea, then unspeakable rage, as I saw a small, crumpled form in the corner of the room. There was no doubt that this form had been Emily; her clothing, though charred, was unmistakably the lovely floral print dress Beatrice had made for her on her birthday. At that moment, my heart shattered, and my mind snapped. The smart thing to do would have been to shoot this thing right there, in the back of the head, but it was not sufficient for me. I needed to do the work with my hands. At that time, and after what I had witnessed...God help me, I needed to FEEL this creature die.

Before I knew it, I had drawn back my sword and was about to thrust it forward into the monster's back when it suddenly turned to face me. Its eyes were a horrid red, and gazing into them directly was near impossible; I had to avert my eyes to keep them from burning. It had several rows of sharp yellow teeth, like a shark, and bellowed at me in some foreign tongue. Its movements seemed to be restricted, however; I noticed that it seemed to be tethered to the walls by a series of tubes that looked like innards. Without hesitation, I plunged my blade into the creature's chest as it shrieked mightily. Pushing with all my might, the sword not only went through the creature, but penetrated the metal wall as well. I felt a strange surge of some unknown force throughout my entire being as the room was illuminated by a blinding flash of light.

For one brief moment that felt like an eternity, the creature wailed, its sickly brown blood running down the shaft of the sword like molasses. Its face looked down into mine as unbridled hate radiated mutually between us. Then I twisted the sword, and slowly extracted it. The creature reached towards me, blood squirting out of its chest as its enormous arm raised. In its massive fist, it held some sort of metal cylinder of unknown purpose. Before it could reach me, however, an explosion emanating from behind the beast shook the entire room. It whipped around toward the strange apparatuses behind it as steam and further explosions rocked the enclosure. Chunks of rocks began falling from the ceiling as fiery bursts and haze filled the small area. Hastily, I scooped up poor Emily and ran from the room. A final unearthly wail from the creature echoed around me as a cave-in sealed the aperture. I rushed outside, but aside from the light tinkle of tiny shards of rock and earth falling to the ground, the cave was silent. Looking down at what remained of my child, I fell to my knees and wept.

The sun was more than halfway below the horizon as I headed back home to deliver the horrid news. I could picture Beatrice's face, and dreaded her reaction to this senseless slaughter. The walk was, as the rest of the day had been, a surreal nightmare. When I did finally reach our doorway, Beatrice opened the door before I could. Though she has wept inconsolably, she has not spoken since. Nor has Thomas, who I have been unable to coax away from the far corner of his room. He merely stares at the wall, perhaps reliving his own nightmare.

I wouldn't know what to say even if they wished to talk. I

have never felt such pain in my entire life. Tomorrow, I bury my daughter.

As Henry finished reading the entry, he closed the journal and placed it at his bedside. Even though he didn't know these people, he was intensely disturbed by what he had read. Either Jeremiah Lee Garrison was a hell of a storyteller in the grand Orson Wells tradition, or something seriously messed-up had happened. Either way, Henry had a hard time getting the image of a young girl's corpse out of his head, and was nearly moved to tears. After several minutes of staring at the floor, he reached over for his backpack and unzipped it to get his homework. His life had become extremely bizarre far too quickly, and he needed some nice, boring normalcy to keep himself sane. Still, as he read about trickle-down economics, he was haunted by images of a dead little girl and a red-eyed monster. He sensed insomnia coming on.

Chapter Four

As Henry and Doug were running laps in PE the next day, Henry blurted out, "I have to show you something."

"If it's your junk, I'll pass," said Doug. "But I'm really flattered."

"Wishful thinking," said Henry. "But no, seriously. It's pretty nuts."

"Interesting choice of words," said Doug. "What is it?"

"You'll see."

"Oh, come on. You can't just leave me hanging like that."

"I'm not going to leave you hanging," said Henry. "You're just going to have to wait until after school."

"Jeez," said Doug. "Fine. It better be good."

"It is, don't worry," said Henry.

"Is it porn?" said Doug.

"What *is* it with you?" said Henry.

After running laps, the class was divided into two teams as softball continued. As usual, Henry was drafted towards the end, before the obese children but after anyone who was actually athletic. He didn't mind; expectations for him were low enough that there was very little pressure. He played the outfield and did an adequate job of fielding, but whenever he came to bat, he was assumed to be an out more often than not.

After striking out in his first at bat, then hitting into a double play on his second, Henry found himself next up to bat with his team down by two runs. They had a runner on second, and a capable batter in Ronnie Gerber currently at the plate. However, they also had two outs, so there was no guarantee Henry would even be hitting. Henry tapped his fingers against the gloves in his pocket; he refused to leave them unattended for a moment, even in a padlocked locker. He watched the at-bat intently.

Doug leaned over from the bench. "So what's this thing you're going to show me?" he asked.

"I told you, you're going to have to wait," said Henry, his

eyes fixed on Ronnie.

"Well, see, it just sounds so bad when you say that," said Doug. "Like you're gonna show me a dead body or something. Like in *Boyz N the Hood.*"

"I assure you, it's nothing like *Boyz N the Hood.*"

"Well then tell me.".

"Damn, you sure are nosy," said Henry. "I shouldn't have told you in the first place."

Ronnie hit a single, and got safely on first base while advancing the runner. It looked like Henry was going to be batting after all. As he rose, he took a single heavy breath and, despite his better judgment, pulled the gloves out of his pocket and put them on.

"Here," he said to Doug. "I'll show you."

Henry grabbed a bat and strode to the plate, the aluminum practically weightless in his hands. This was a terrible, awful idea. He wasn't ready for this. And yet, he couldn't help himself. Squinting, he grinned at the pitcher, and settled into his usual awkward batting stance. Somehow, despite the secret he has keeping, he felt less anxious than usual.

The first pitch whizzed past Henry as he flailed at it. His movements were definitely faster, his reflexes enhanced, compared to his usual hitting, but he was not used to it, and thus grossly miscalculated his swing. Additionally, his swing was so much more powerful than usual, it was too hard; the sheer force it generated actually knocked over the pitcher, much to his confusion. No one equated the swing and the fall, though; not even the pitcher. Everyone just assumed he had slipped, perhaps due to careless groundskeeping. It was the only explanation that made sense.

Doug gave Henry a thumbs-up from the bench. "Great secret," he mouthed.

On his second swing, Henry held back considerably. His timing was off and his swing was awful, and he was embarrassed at his second strike. The other players on his team were yelling at him now; if he screwed this up, they had lost their chance at a comeback. Unfortunately, the gloves gave him power and speed, but it remained up to Henry to provide the actual talent.

Snorting, Henry narrowed his focus and dug the tip of his

shoe into the dirt at home plate. This was ridiculous. Gripping the bat even tighter in annoyance, he could feel the gauze within his glove rubbing against his singed palm. As the ball came towards him, he unleashed his pain and frustration upon it.

The force of Henry's swing once again knocked over the pitcher, but this time, no one was looking at the pitcher. They were looking at the ball, which vanished. More accurately, it was hit obscenely far, and everyone watched it while it sailed not only over the back fence, but over rooftops, and into the aether. It was launched so authoritatively, such an unimaginable distance, that no one on the field had ever seen anything like it. Red-faced, Henry jogged around the bases, careful not to run too fast. His team screamed in jubilation as he rounded the bases and headed home.

"That's some good hitting, Garrison," said Coach Grisham, who sipped out of his thermos and winced a bit. "Damn good."

"Oh my God," said Doug. "What the hell was that? How did you do that?"

"I'll explain it later. Don't worry," said Henry. As the rest of the team approached him for hi-fives, and to gush over the sheer force of his home run, he slipped off his gloves, turned back to Doug and said, "I told you it was gonna be good."

In economics class, Henry couldn't help but faze out Ms. Tegg explained laissez-faire. He scribbled in his notebook, drawing a stick figure lifting up an enormous boulder, and writing in the margins: "Step 1: Acquire superpowers. Step 2: ???. Step 3: Profit!"

Denise Hargrove leaned over and whispered, "I heard you hit a crazy home run this morning."

Briefly confused, Henry cocked his head and replied, "Who, me? Yeah. I did."

"Huh," said Denise. "How'd you do that?"

"I hit the ball. I don't know."

"Hmm," said Denise. "That's cool. I wish I had seen it."

"Well, maybe next time."

Denise looked at Henry for a second more, then turned her attention back to the class. Henry glanced over at her, then went back to scribbling. Almost unconsciously, he drew a dark cave, with a pair of sinister eyes glaring out of the blackness.

"So what was that all about?" said Doug after school, as he and Henry walked off campus. He had waited around for Henry to get out of detention because he absolutely needed to know what was going on. "I've never seen anybody hit a ball like that. What, have you been taking hitting classes from Barry Bonds or something? Is that what it is?"

"No," said Henry. "Something happened to me. I'm...a little bit different than I used to be."

"Yeah, obviously," said Doug.

"I'm...well, I'm really, really strong now," said Henry. "If you want to come with me, I'll show you what I mean. I don't really want to do anything in front of all these other guys."

"Mmm-hmm," said Doug. "But you'll hit a ridiculous home run in front of everybody in P.E."

"Yeah, I probably shouldn't have done that," said Henry sheepishly. "I mean, everybody will know eventually, probably. But for now, I should probably keep this to my inner circle."

"Everybody already knows, dude. I've been asked about the

home run like thirty times today. Don't tell me no one's asked *you* about it."

"Yeah, OK," said Henry. "But that could've just been a lucky hit. It'll blow over. When I really show people what I can do, it'll make all that look like nothing."

"This is really weird," said Doug. "You're not taking me somewhere to kill me, are you?"

"Do you really think I would do that?"

"Probably not," said Doug. "But I didn't think you were going to hit a softball into the stratosphere, either."

"Well, I promise, I'm not taking you somewhere to kill you. Or torture or maim you, just to get that out of the way."

"OK," said Doug. "I see softball isn't the only time you cover your bases."

"Ugh," Henry groaned.

As the pair walked toward the woods, they didn't talk much. Doug looked somewhat pale and nervous, and Henry kept looking over at him, but didn't say anything. Finally, Doug said, "So what's really going on? You're messing with me, right? 'Cause I don't..."

"No," said Henry. "I'm dead friggin' serious here."

The pair reached the clearing, and Doug zipped up his sweatshirt and tucked his hands into its pockets. Henry looked around and, not seeing anyone else, picked up a stone and showed it to Doug.

"Look," he said, then nonchalantly crushed it to dust.

"What the hell?" said Doug. "What was...?"

"No, no, look," said Henry. He walked over to the tree he had punched through one his last trip here. "I made this hole with my bare hands. Honestly."

"No way," said Doug.

Sighing, Henry gripped the tree and braced himself. He dug his fingers into the bark and strained, then ripped the tree from the ground with a grunt. Sweating a bit, he held it aloft over his head, then grinned at Doug, whose face was a milky white.

"How did you do that?" he stammered. "I mean, jeez, Henry, that's not possible."

"I'm telling you, man," said Henry, setting the tree down. "Something happened to me. I can do this stuff now. Don't expect me to explain it, but there it is."

"Damn, dude," said Doug, "when did this happen?"

Henry had decided that he was going to be as vague about his powers as possible. He was under no circumstances going to tell anyone that the power came from the gloves; that would just be an invitation for anyone and everyone to try and steal them from him. That also meant that he was going to have to make a conscious effort to be nonchalant about putting them on or removing them; if he was too obvious, someone would figure it out, and he simply couldn't have that.

"Maybe a few days ago," said Henry. "It was the weirdest freaking thing. I just sort of ...got stronger. I wish I had a better explanation than that, but really, it's pretty bizarre. I don't understand it myself, but I'm not really going to look a gift horse in the mouth."

"I guess not," said Doug. "What are you gonna do, then? Not keep it a secret, obviously."

"No," said Henry. "I'm not really sure. I have to figure it out, I guess. But it's gonna be awesome, man."

"For sure," said Doug. "So, wait, is there anything else you can do? I mean, can you fly or anything?"

"Well, I tried that, but no, I can't fly," said Henry. "But, but wait. Check this out." He leapt up in the air, soaring even higher than he had the last time. He landed more or less gracefully, stumbling slightly but landing on his feet.

"Holy mother of God!" said Doug. "Didn't that hurt? I mean you were, what, a hundred feet up? More?"

"No...that's the weird thing," said Henry. "Well, one of the weird things. I guess there's a few. But yeah, doesn't hurt. Hell, I smacked into a tree the other day and didn't even get a scratch. It's crazy."

"Wow," said Doug. "I have to admit, this is just...well, you were right, this is pretty cool. Hey, can you crush another rock?"

"Sure," said Henry.

The scythe was still laying on Henry's floor. He kept the bedroom door locked at all times, so there was no real chance of anyone stumbling in on it, and its constant blue glow made the weapon very easy to avoid in the course of a trip to the bathroom in the middle of the night. Nonetheless, Henry was uncomfortable with the idea of just leaving it on the floor; the trouble was, he couldn't bring himself to touch it. The very thought of it made his hand throb. So when he got back home that night, he stepped over the scythe and sit down on his bed, grabbing Jeremiah's journal and flipping to where he had left off.

August 20, 1888

Beatrice finally talked to me this morning; Thomas, however, remained despondent. A dark cloud clearly hangs over our house. Yet despite the bizarre and tragic events of the past few days, I have made another peculiar discovery, perhaps even more unbelievable than those before it.

Having buried Emily, I could not help but think of the foul creature that slaughtered my poor daughter. I assumed it had perished amidst the explosions or the subsequent cave-in, but as I really had no idea what sort of beast I was dealing with, I had no real way of knowing for certain. Therefore, I decided to take some dynamite and seal the cave completely, in order to ensure that the evil was forever sealed within, dead or alive. Kissing Beatrice, I put on my gloves and coat and headed back into the hills.

I confess feeling very strange on the way there. However, I have felt strange in various ways ever since Emily's disappearance, so this was not in and of itself unusual. It was a different sort of strange, to be sure, but I tried not to overly concern myself with it. I found it quite odd, though, that the dynamite in my hands felt weightless. I began to wonder if perhaps I had suffered some sort of nerve damage during the encounter in the cave.

Upon reaching the cave, I felt an irresistible urge to go inside; my morbid curiosity compelled me to revisit the site of the earlier tragedy. Slowly and carefully, I approached the part of the cave that had held the creature, and sure enough, found it to be utterly covered over by rocks and earth; there was no trace of the monster or his metal room. Well, almost no trace. I did happen to find, barely visible amidst the debris, the yellow cylinder the creature had been holding shortly before the explosions started. I picked it up and stared at it, unable to discern exactly what it was, my hate growing as memories of the beast flooded back. Unthinking, I lashed out, and punched at the rubble with my left hand. I certainly did not expect what happened next.

My fist smashed deep into the pile of rocks, pulverizing them as my arm effortlessly sunk in up to my armpit. The rock gave way like a wall of cobwebs, and there was not the slightest bit of discomfort in my hand. Amazed but terrified, I extracted my arm and backed away. After standing still for a moment, I slipped the cylinder into my coat pocket and picked up a stone from the ground. As I gripped it in my hand, it cracked and exploded into dust. I tested this several times with the same result. As I picked up one stone, I noticed a stain on it that, on closer inspection, appeared to be blood. The sight of it made me lose control. I smashed the walls and ceiling of the cave to pieces with my bare hands. Like a wild man, I did not stop until there was no cave left at all, merely rubble. I am not sure anything in Heaven or Earth could have stopped me.

Having utterly buried the cave, I sat outside and gathered my thoughts. None of what was happening made any sense, and I suspected it never would. While I sat, I examined the cylinder and got yet another shock: by depressing a certain section of it, it somehow transformed into a scythe. A fitting weapon, I suppose, given its original bearer. I cannot explain how such a thing would be possible, how such a large object could fit into such a small space, but the weapon folded in upon itself again with another depression. As sickening as I find it, I cannot bring myself to discard or destroy the scythe. In truth, I doubt I could destroy it even if I tried.

I do not know from where my newfound strength originates, nor how to broach the topic to my family. For now, I will simply write, and hope this all makes sense later. In a way, this power makes Emily's death all the more tragic, for here I am, able to lift up an oak, but useless as Gaines's army when my daughter's life was in danger.

Henry's first thought when he finished reading this entry was that apparently, crushing rocks was a fairly standard test of newfound superpowers. He wondered if Jeremiah had figured out at this point that the gloves were the source of the power, but little in the journal seemed to indicate this. Furthermore, he gave no indication of the scythe causing him bodily harm, so either its properties had changed over time, or the gloves had protected him from it. Looking at the gleaming blade on his floor, Henry couldn't help but shudder at the thought that it had originally belonged to some otherworldly, murderous creature. He needed to put it away. Time to test his theory, he supposed.

Pulling the gloves on, he stood above the scythe, his innards bubbling with anxiety. Sucking on his teeth, he leaned down slowly and gripped the shaft of the scythe. Nothing. No pain, no burning. Heaving an immense sigh of relief, he pushed the emerald button and watched the weapon fold back into its cylindrical form instantaneously. He put the cylinder back into the old wooden box, which lay open and empty beneath his bed. He then pushed the box back into its pseudo-hiding place and sat back down on the bed.

He continued reading Jeremiah's journal, and learned a number of interesting things. Jeremiah soon figured out that the power came from the gloves, and also that touching the gloves together deactivated them. Henry tested this, and found it to be true, making a mental note to be careful while clapping in the future. Apparently, Jeremiah had parlayed his extraordinary abilities into a sort of sideshow, for lack of a better term, where people paid money to see him perform seemingly impossible feats of strength. Considering the lack of television back then, this was a lucrative business plan, and eventually provided Jeremiah with enough money to purchase the very house Henry now lived in (good lord, it was even older than he thought). Eventually, Henry got bored with the journal; the entries became fairly mundane, with the occasional wistful reference to Emily. He set it aside, resolving to finish it at some later point just in case there was anything else particularly interesting or important in there. He then turned his attention to his homework, the completion of which was slowed considerably by his daydreams of punching through walls and bounding over rooftops. He just barely finished by 2 AM.

That Saturday, Henry had gathered Doug, Trent, and Albert, after filling in the latter two on just what was going on with him. Their initial disbelief was not assuaged by Doug's reassurances; Trent actually got more annoyed at what he perceived as a needlessly elaborate and transparent attempt to make him look foolish. Nonetheless, the four of them headed to the park that lay at the exact center of St. Dante, at Henry's request. When they got there, Henry walked over to the large bronze statue of Thaddeus "Kodiak" Worthington, the town founder, and said with a carnival barker's grin, "Gentlemen, what you are about to see will be utterly unbelievable for you. You may, at times, think you are having a dream, or experiencing mass hysteria, or perhaps some sort of drug-induced hallucination. But I assure you, this is real. There is no trickery involved here. This..."

"Get on with it," said Trent. "I'm hungry."

"Alright," said Henry. "But before I do this...Doug, let me remind you that I have given you the phone number for our friendly local television news organization."

"Got it," Doug said, rolling his eyes.

"Then here we go. We're gonna be rich," said Henry. He gripped the statue around the base with his gloved hands and took a few preparatory breaths. He leaned over, reminding himself to lift with his legs and, one surge of adrenaline later, the statue was lifted above his head. It was heavy, and definitely a strain on him, but it was nothing he couldn't handle. "Tah-dah," he said.

"Jesus Christ," said Trent, taking a couple of steps backwards.

"I told you," said Doug.

Albert didn't say anything. But from the look on his face, he seemed impressed. So did everyone in the vicinity; a number of people saw what was going on and came over to observe up close, flabbergasted.

"I got the idea from an episode of *The Twilight Zone*," Henry said. "Burgess Meredith got super strength, and he basically did this to get fame and fortune."

"Huh," said Trent. "And what happened?"

"Um, the invisible aliens who gave him the super strength took it back from him, and he was humiliated. He had to go back to being a normal person, and was miserable," said Henry. "That's not really the end result I'm going for, but the basic premise seemed sound."

"Have you ever considered that maybe invisible aliens gave you your powers, and they're going to take them back?" said Doug. "Because that would really suck for you."

"I've thought about it," said Henry. "I just really don't think it's very likely."

"I think 'likely' kind of goes out the window when you're holding a huge bronze statue over your head," said Doug.

"Good point," said Albert.

"OK, so could you call the TV station, Doug?" said Henry. "I'm not doing this for my own personal amusement. Well, not entirely."

"Yeah, yeah," said Doug, pulling his cell phone out of his pocket.

"What are you doing?" a middle-aged brunette woman asked as she scooted up to Henry. "Is this one of those magic tricks? Like David Blaine?"

"I assure you, this is nothing like David Blaine," said Henry.

"Yeah, but are you going to make the statue disappear or

something?" said a thirty-something man in a polo shirt and khakis.

"No, I'm not going to make anything disappear," said Henry. "I don't think you get it. I'm actually lifting this up. Honest."

"Can I take a picture?" said another woman. Quite a crowd was beginning to form.

"Sure," said Henry. "Knock yourself out."

"I can see the strings," said the man in the polo shirt, leaning over to another man. "See, look, right there. You can kind of see the light bouncing off them."

"Oh yeah," said the other man, squinting. "I think I can see them too."

"No, you can't," said Henry. "There aren't any strings. Besides, what kind of strings could hold up a statue? Seriously!" His increasing annoyance made the statue feel heavier, and he grunted and shifted his weight underneath it.

"Maybe that's not the real statue," said the polo shirted man. "Maybe that's a fake, made out of styrofoam. Why, I could lift that!"

"You could lift it? You could lift it?" asked Henry, his face flushed. He placed the statue back on the ground, considerably more forcefully than he intended to. "Then lift it. Go ahead."

The man walked up to the statue and looked back at the meager crowd. Then he turned to the statue, adopted a wide-leg stance, and tried to yank it off the ground. A muffled squeal snuck out of his nose and through his clenched teeth. Panting, he stood up straight and turned around.

"It's real," he said, then stood back beside his friend, his face red as raw beef.

The crowd applauded politely and congratulated Henry on a wonderful trick. As he tried to plead his case, the people dispersed. Soon, it was just Henry and his friends.

"Damn skeptics," said Henry. "I swear, special effects have ruined it for everybody."

"Everybody being the large population with superpowers, right?" said Trent.

"Did you call the TV station?" said Henry, turning to Doug. "Maybe I can still get on the news."

"Yeah, I called them," said Doug. "They laughed at me and hung up."

Chapter Five

Henry had a plan. If you could call it that. He decided that a single spectacular display of strength was not enough to gain him any sort of notoriety; if he was going to get people's attention, this was going to have to become a lifestyle. He was going to have to perform a steady stream of seemingly impossible acts in order to make an impact. Then maybe the television networks would come calling, and he would be able to make some serious money.

In addition, Henry decided to wear the gloves at all times, except in the shower and other such exceptions. If his strength obviously came and went, it might seem suspicious enough that someone could potentially figure out that the gloves were the source of his power. The downside to this course of action was that Henry would have to provide a satisfactory explanation as to why he was suddenly wearing gloves all the time. In order to combat this, Henry came up with the idea of wearing a uniform of sorts.

There was no way he was going to adopt a spandex suit in the fine superhero tradition, due to the fact that the cyclist or professional rollerblader look did not exactly scream "icon." Besides, it was cost prohibitive. Instead, he went to the mall and had his black hooded sweatshirt monogrammed for $18. Now, across his back it read "HENRY GARRISON" in large red letters. He told the nice Asian woman who did the monogramming that he would be back to have some t-shirts made once he had some more money. That might be more prudent attire once the weather warmed up and it became a chore to wear a sweatshirt all the time. In any case, he had his uniform, slapdash though it was.

In P.E. class on Monday morning, Henry strode out of the locker room with his sweatshirt and gloves on in addition to his normal uniform. Today they were playing soccer, and he was eager to try out his abilities on the field. At roll call, Coach Grisham ambled down the line of students and stopped at Henry.

"That sweatshirt's not regulation, Garrison," he said. "I'm gonna have to dock you a few points."

"It's school colors, though," said Henry. "Black and red,

see? And I'm cold."

"It's not regulation," said Coach Grisham. He took a long sip from his thermos which, as usual, was not steaming even in the frigid morning air. "It's the rules. Have to dock ya."

"OK," said Henry, shrugging. "If it's the rules."

"So you wore the pee clothes, but won't take your vanity sweatshirt off," said Doug. "I have to question the logic there."

"If I'm going to build a brand here, I'm going to have to market myself," said Henry.

"Ah, yes," said Doug. "The great, untapped P.E. class market."

During the soccer game, Henry struggled. Specifically, he struggled to reign in his speed. He knew that if he pushed himself, he would likely run into someone, and considering the damage he had done to the tree he had run into, he didn't want to see what effects a collision might have on a human body. This led him to playing very awkwardly, at a strange pace somewhere between running and walking, and hoping that this would get easier as he got used to these powers. Eventually, despite this, he found himself with the ball and a clear shot on the goal, and kicked the ball with a considerable amount of force. The goalie, Ronnie Gerber, threw himself in front of the ball. It connected with his left shoulder, and he wailed and crumpled. Henry began to wish he was as cautious with his kick as he had been with his running.

"They're saying it's probably a fracture," said Mr. Sadek. "I don't really enjoy having to tell a student's parents that he was seriously injured during one of his classes. It does not reflect well on the school and it does not reflect well on me."

"I'm sorry," said Henry, leaning back in the hideous brown plastic chair. "I apologized to Ronnie. I didn't mean to hurt him...it just happened."

"Yes, well, I'm making sure it doesn't happen again," said Mr. Sadek, pushing his glasses up the bridge of his nose. "I've been hearing things about you lately, Henry. I don't really know what to make of them."

"What kind of things?" said Henry.

"Strange things," said Mr. Sadek, taking a sip of coffee.

"Things I don't know if I believe. But after what happened today, I think it's for the best that you...not go back to P.E. class."

"What?"

"It's just...I need to protect my students, Henry. And I don't know what's going on with you, but I think to be on the safe side, you should no longer attend P.E."

"But don't I need to pass it to graduate?"

"Well, yes, technically," said Mr. Sadek. "So here's what we're going to do...I'm passing you. The last thing I need is a discrimination complaint, so...you're fine. Just sleep in or something. Don't worry about it. Just please, be more careful. I can't be dealing with injured students. I know this wasn't intentional, but...no more, OK?"

"Yeah...OK, I guess," said Henry. "So I just don't go to P.E. anymore?"

"No. Please," said Mr. Sadek. "As a personal favor to the man that is allowing you to effortlessly pass the class."

"Alright," said Henry, rising from the chair. "Thanks...?"

"Mm," said Mr. Sadek.

As Henry walked towards the door, Mr. Sadek cleared his throat.

"Henry?" he said.

"Yes?"

"Can you...did you really lift a statue?"

Henry stood before his parents and grandmother in the living room. He wrung his hands and paced as he tried to piece together exactly what to say. Finally, he turned toward them and folded his hands behind his back.

"So I have something to tell you guys," he said slowly. "It's going to sound really weird, and you may not believe me at first. But I assure you, I'm being completely honest with you, and despite the initial weirdness, I'm pretty sure this is a good thing."

"I'm not sure I like where this is going," said Henry's mother.

"Did you get in trouble at school again?" said Henry's father.

"Well, yes, sort of, but that's not what this is about," said

Henry. "What I'm-"

"What did you do now?" said Henry's mother. "I can't believe you're getting in trouble again...I just-"

"Mom, please," said Henry. "Let me finish. Trust me, this is important."

"I just don't understand why you're getting in all this trouble lately," said Henry's mother. "Maybe it's something in the water."

"I think you're kind of blowing it out of proportion. It's not like I'm doing drugs or killing anybody. And besides, you drink the water too."

"I drink bottled water. Anyway, what did you do this time?"

Henry sighed, "I might have fractured a guy's shoulder. But please, let me explain before you go all nuts."

"Oh my God, Henry," said his mother. "You-"

"Mom, *please*," said Henry. "Just give me a second. Let me finish."

"Fine," she said, crossing her arms.

"There's no easy way to say this, so here goes," said Henry.

"I have superpowers."

The room was silent. Henry's parents shifted uncomfortably. His grandmother smiled slightly, but didn't say anything.

"Now, I know it sounds nuts, but I can prove it to you," said Henry. "Name something heavily. Like, ridiculously heavy. I'll lift it, just watch me."

"Henry...," said his father.

"We're concerned about you," said his mother. "Maybe you should talk to a school counselor or..."

"Mom! I am not talking to a damn school counselor!" said Henry. "I'm not delusional. I'm not disturbed. This is one hundred percent true, and if you just let me show you..."

"No, Henry. Just...no," said his mother. "I don't know what this is all about, but I don't want to encourage it and-"

"We think you're acting like an idiot, son," said his father. "This is idiotic. You do not have superpowers. No one has superpowers."

"No one...*but* me," said Henry. "That's what I'm trying to

tell you. It's very unusual, I understand."

"Henry, I don't get what's going on with you. Between the detention and the..."

Henry walked over to the fireplace, grabbed the iron poker, and bent it in half as though it were a blade of grass. "You see?" he said. "How could I do that if I wasn't really, *really* strong all of a sudden?"

"Oh, great," said his father. "Now we're going to have to buy a new poker."

"No, no, no," said Henry, unbending the poker. "There. Do you see, now?"

"Was that some kind of magic trick?" said his father. "That was pretty good."

"You know what, never mind," said Henry. "I cannot believe that you think I'm making this up." He stormed out the front door, ajar due to the warmth of the late afternoon, fortunately neglecting to slam it.

"We should get that water tested," said his mother.

Henry's eyes narrowed in frustration as he stomped down

the street, unthinkingly leaving cracks in the sidewalk. He shoved his hands in the pockets of his sweatshirt and sighed. When he first discovered his powers, it had been so exciting. And, in a way, it still was. But Henry had been overwhelmed by dreams of fame and fortune, compliments of his marvelous new gift. The future had seemed so bright, his meal ticket was written, and so forth. In reality, however, it seemed that the applications for his talents were far more limited than he had imagined. As he headed into the woods, he became more and more consumed with the urge to smash whatever inanimate objects he could find.

Lost in thought, Henry walked right into someone's chest. Surprisingly, the person didn't stagger or even really move at all; instead, Henry took a step back, stunned.

"Oh my God," said Henry. "I'm so sorry. I wasn't really paying attention...I didn't see you."

"Hmm," said the man.

Henry looked up at this man, and felt uneasy. The man was huge, probably 6'6", with shoulder-length hair that had seemingly once been jet black but was now laden with silver strands, piercing gray eyes, and a neck like a tree trunk. He was pale bur not at all sickly, and wore a long black coat that was buttoned all the way up and a pair of remarkably clean boots. He had a smile so faint, it seemed illusory.

"Yeah, sorry. Sorry," said Henry, walking around the man's side while continuing to face him. "I'll just be...yeah, sorry."

As Henry hastily turned and walked away, red-faced, the man simply stood there, silent, staring. Once Henry was a hundred or so feet away, he turned and looked behind him. The man was still there, having not moved a muscle, watching him. A shiver ran down Henry's spine as he continued to walk. After another fifty feet or so, he looked behind him again. Nothing was there but trees, and a few autumn leaves rustling in the wind.

Henry trekked to the clearing in the woods but, finding half a dozen teenagers hanging out there smoking hand-rolled cigarettes and drinking something out of a paper bag, he called Doug to see if he was home. He was, so Henry walked over to his house. After some fresh baked chocolate chip cookies courtesy of Doug's mother, Henry headed up to Doug's room and knocked on the door. He knew better than to walk into a teenage male's room unannounced.

"I'm kind of at a loss," said Henry a few minutes later, sitting on Doug's bed. "I don't really know what to do with myself. I feel like I'm wasting this...whatever it is. Basically, I have an amazing gift that I have no practical use for, and I'm getting really frustrated."

"It's kind of like you have a million dollars, but it's in store credit for that place that sells nothing but t-shirts with cartoon dogs on them," said Doug, who was sitting in a chair at his desk.

"Yes," said Henry, pointing at Doug. "That's far more accurate than any simile I could have come up with."

"It's what I do," said Doug.

"So what do you think?" said Henry. "I should be using this to get rich and famous, but how can I do that?"

"Well, there's the internet," said Doug. "Make some videos of yourself, I don't know, tossing heavy crap around, and post them up online. That could get you a global audience, conceivably."

"Yeah, but here's the thing," said Henry, "people can't even believe that what I'm doing isn't some sort of trick when it's happening right in front of their faces. If I put a video up online, everyone is going to think it's special effects. Computer generated or whatever. No one would possibly take it as fact."

"You've got a point," said Doug, chewing on the end of a ball-point pen. "You could go into some sort of fighting tournament, like MMA or something."

"That's kind of sketchy, though," said Henry. "I feel like that would be really unfair, like I would be cheating." He also was concerned that the promotion wouldn't let him wear his gloves in a fight, or find some other way to expose the source of his powers, and there was no way he was going to risk that.

Doug grunted. "Well, maybe fame and fortune are not in the cards for you. I mean, basically, you're an amped-up version of one of those dudes that can pull a truck with his teeth, and they're only on TV once a year for strongman competitions. Maybe you're just not marketable."

"But no one else can do what I do. I'm unique."

"So is that guy that squirts milk out of his eyes," said Doug. "Wanna play *Street Fighter* or something?"

"...Yeah."

At school on Monday, Henry was between classes, swinging his lunch box perhaps a bit more than he intended, when a familiar voice froze him in his tracks.

"Nice outfit, Garrison." said Roderick. "It really captures a sense of, 'Hey, I'm a jerk-off.'"

"Coming from the king of the jerk-offs," Henry said without turning around, "that's pretty high praise."

"Oh ho ho," said Roderick, walking in front of Henry. "Cute. Listen, I've been meaning to talk to you. This whole 'I need attention' kick you're on lately is pretty pathetic, honestly. I don't know what you're trying to do, but nobody cares."

"Wow, hey, thanks for saving me from myself, buddy. I owe you."

"No, really though," said Roderick, putting his face right in front of Henry's, "what are you trying to do? You've got your stupid sweatshirt, you put Ronnie in a cast, now I hear you're banned from P.E. class or something? What are you, some kind of badass all of a sudden? Am I supposed to be *scared*?"

Henry scowled. "What if I am?"

"You are, and always have been, a loser," said Roderick. "But I didn't know you were a psycho too."

"Whatever, man," said Henry. "Seriously, just get out of my way."

"Oh, am I inconveniencing you?" Roderick snarled, then snatched Henry's shirt collar. Or at least tried to.

Before Roderick could get a grip of Henry, Henry had grabbed Roderick by the collar and hoisted him up with one hand. "Look, I'm going to tell you this once," said Henry. "Stay the hell out of my face."

Shocked and stammering, Roderick flailed at Henry ineffectually. After a few pathetic moments, Roderick coughed and hissed, "What are you gonna do? Kill me?" Then he emitted some sort of gasping chuckle, still suspended above the ground.

Before Henry could say anything, he heard someone yelling.

He turned and saw Coach Grisham approaching him, and dropped Roderick, who immediately adjusted his collar.

"Garrison! What the hell do you think you're doing?"

"Um, I..."

"Yeah," said Roderick, "what the hell *do* you think you're doing?"

"Hey, he was harassing me," said Henry. "He was getting in my face and saying all kinds of stuff."

"This school has a zero tolerance policy for violence," said Coach Grisham. "You could be suspended for this, Garrison. Maybe even expelled."

"Hey, I'm sorry. It's not like I hit him or anything...I was just trying to get him to back off."

Sighing, Coach Grisham said, "You're lucky I don't tell Mr. Sadek about this. You better simmer down, Garrison. I'm not going to let anything like this fly, you understand me? This is the no-fly zone, and I'm the, uh…the, uh, commander. Of it."

"Yeah, I understand. I think."

"Good. I'm watching you."

As Coach Grisham walked off, shaking his head, Roderick laughed. "How sad. I give it a week before you're expelled."

"Kiss my ass, Roderick," said Henry. As he turned to walk away, Roderick yelled after him.

"Don't think you're going to get away with touching me. No way in hell."

"I can't believe this," said Henry, cracking open his bottle of Yoo-Hoo at lunch. "Now I almost get suspended because of Roderick. This is ridiculous."

"I wish I could have seen it," said Trent. "I bet half the school would love to see him get his ass kicked."

"Yeah, well, it wasn't very impressive," said Henry. "I just lifted him up. I wanted to scare him. It really wasn't worth it."

"Are you sure?" said Trent.

"OK, maybe it sort of was," said Henry. "Oh, and he told me I'm not going to get away with it, so I guess he's going to get his revenge or something."

"Try not to lose too much sleep over that," said Doug.

"Jenny told me that Roderick is going to the Halloween dance with Denise Hargrove," said Albert, taking a sip of Coke.

"Wait, what?" said Henry. "Are you serious?"

"Hey, they're both popular," said Albert. "It makes sense."

"I guess," said Henry. "But...eww. Why?"

"Aww, sorry champ," said Doug. "But hey, you never know. Maybe she has an irresistible attraction to guys who smell like the gym bathroom that will lead her right back to you."

"That is so ridiculously not funny," said Henry.

"I don't know, it kind of is," said Trent.

"Hey, she asked about my home run the other day," Henry said. "Just out of nowhere."

"Well, let's book the honeymoon suite," said Doug.

"Whatever," said Henry.

"So what should I wear to the dance?" said Albert. "I'm not really sure."

"Yeah, like we all have an intense familiarity with your wardrobe," said Trent.

"Tuxedo, definitely," said Doug. "Preferably a powder blue

one."

"Vinyl jumpsuit," said Henry.

"I seriously don't know why I hang out with you guys," said Albert.

After his usual daily detention, Henry walked home, hands in his pockets. A sharp autumn wind whipped around him, but he could not feel the slightest breeze. He thought about Roderick and Denise, and felt his face warm. How could anyone, let alone Denise, like Roderick at all? It was just unfathomable to him. Sure, Roderick had a ridiculous amount of money, and certainly a lot of confidence, and under excruciating torture, Henry might even have admitted that he wasn't a bad looking guy. Nonetheless, his personality made Irritable Bowel Syndrome seem appealing by comparison. Maybe he acted differently among other people.

Henry's thoughts were disrupted by a scream. He wasn't sure where it had come from, but he knew he had heard it. He stopped and scanned the area to see if he could see anything wrong. For a few moments, there was nothing but silence. Then he heard a cacophony of unpleasantness, somewhat distant, but close enough to be especially disturbing. There were multiple screams now, male and female, mixed with profanity and some loud cracking and booming sounds. Whatever was causing the commotion, there was zero chance of it being pleasant. His heart pounding, Henry started to back away from the noise and contemplate the quickest route he could take to make his way home. Then he caught himself. He was extremely strong and fast, and if not invincible, he was certainly more difficult to hurt than your average brick wall. There was no reason why he shouldn't at least take a look at whatever was going on. As people began to pour towards him, oblivious to his presence in their terrified haste to escape whatever was creating the awful din, Henry pushed himself forward toward God knows what.

As he got closer to the racket, Henry realized that, with the strength of his jumps, it might be wise to take the high ground, so he leapt onto the nearest rooftop. His knees nearly buckled as he caught sight of the source of the noise.

An enormous beast the likes of which Henry had never seen was attacking downtown St. Dante. It was a reddish-purple, like a bruise, and had the elongated, limbless body of a serpent. However, it was far larger than any serpent Henry had ever seen or imagined. At least two hundred feet long, the beast's thick body snaked in between buildings and coiled around lampposts. Its head was the size of an SUV, with piercing orange eyes and teeth like stalactites, and its back was lined with crooked black spines. Most of the people in the area had fled, but the streets were littered with flipped cars and broken glass. The creature bellowed, an eerie bark emanating from its cavernous maw.

Henry nearly lost control of his bladder. Balling his hands up into fists, he staggered backwards in horror. What was this thing? Where had it come from? It was something out of myth, like a dragon or perhaps a dinosaur, but how could such a thing exist in this day and age? Henry began to rethink his urge to charge in and help. But as he stood there, watching the beast decimate a chunk of his hometown, Henry thought of his family, his friends, his acquaintances who weren't quite his friends but whom he had a certain degree of fondness for. If this creature's rampage continued, they might all be hurt, or killed. If there was any chance he might be able to do something about it, then damn it, he should. Still, the prospect was beyond terrifying.

Taking a deep breath, Henry took off his backpack and placed it and his lunch box onto the roof. He then dashed and leaped from rooftop to rooftop until he was less than twenty feet away from the monster. Despite the rapid onset of cottonmouth, he swallowed hard and called out to it.

"Hey!" he hollered. "You mind knocking that off?"

The serpent turned and faced Henry, its jaws inches away. Acrid breath flooded from its cavernous nostrils, gagging Henry with the stench of a violently disturbed crypt. Henry froze up briefly, but as those teeth neared him, he swung his fists wildly in panicked defense. He connected with a hard right hook against the creature's leathery flesh, and its head whipped away sharply. Snarling, the creature reared up and swung its head back like a cobra ready to strike. Its enormous eyes narrowed as it sized Henry up. Then, like lightning, it darted forward with its jaws open wide. Henry barely sprang out of the way as the beast's head smashed into the roof. Concrete bits rained down as Henry hit the street, looking for cover. If he was going to try to fight this thing, he had to figure out a plan of some sort.

Henry ran away from the creature's bulbous head, towards its cylindrical body. As soon as he reached it, he began to assault the tough flesh, which was far slimier than he had anticipated. Henry's fists slipped and skidded along the wet, slick flesh. It was like trying to punch out a waterfall, like fighting someone with Vaseline smeared all over themselves. A gargantuan someone. In his frustration, Henry failed to notice the creature's head swinging down and slamming into him, sending him flying through a store window.

Stunned, Henry lay in a pile of glass and debris on the store floor. Bags of cheese-flavored puffed snacks crunched under his fingers as he pushed himself up. The moment he reached his feet, he yelped as he saw the monster's open jaws shooting toward him as its head busted through the remains of the store wall. Henry barely dodged it and jumped past the head, out the shattered window. As he left, the ceiling caved in on top of the creature. It reared up, barely fazed. This was not going well at all.

Deciding that assaulting the beast's body was more trouble than it was worth, Henry focused on its head. He grabbed a chunk of broken concrete and hurled it straight at the monster's left eye. It missed, but slammed right into the creature's temple. The beast reared back and shook its head and, sensing an opening, Henry launched himself right at the injured spot. He landed a solid punch right where the concrete chunk had busted open the creature's flesh. Blood, thick and brown like castor oil, smeared on Henry's gloves as the impact of the blow sent the monster's head crashing down on top of an upside-down convertible.

His feet hitting the pavement a few feet away, Henry pressed his advantage and ran straight at the monster. It whipped its head out of the way moments before Henry could reach it, then snapped it back and slammed it into him, catching him off-balance. This time, Henry flew right into one of the beast's coils, which quickly wrapped around his body. The wall of slimy flesh closing in on him, Henry gasped and strained. Fortunately, between the slipperiness of the creature's skin and the teflon-like protection the gloves granted him, Henry managed to wriggle out. Unfortunately, while he was focused on this, he ignored the fact that the creature's open maw was rushing toward him. Everything went dark as massive jaws closed around him.

Henry patted himself down in the murky, warm blackness. On the plus side, he had avoided the teeth, and was thus still in one piece. On the minus side, the inside of the monster's mouth smelled like someone had emptied out a slaughterhouse onto their front lawn and left it in the sun to fester for a few weeks. The humid air within the mouth was nearly unbreatheable, which would have been a more serious concern for Henry were it not for the fact that the creature was swallowing, and its muscle spasms were forcing him down the slick tunnel of its throat. As the contractions of the moist wall of flesh tugged Henry down toward oblivion, he panicked. He screamed and lashed out violently, striking the flesh with punches and kicks. But he had no leverage, and though the creature shuddered, Henry could still feel himself pulled down, down, as if he were standing in a pool of particularly foul-smelling quicksand. Desperately, he clawed at the walls, trying to get a grip on something, anything. Finally, though his fingers slipped, he managed to get a hold of some sort of tissue. Feeling faint but determined not to die, he reached up and sunk his fingers in, getting another grip at the expense of the creature's innards. Grimly, he pulled himself up, handful by handful, fighting desperately to stay conscious and sane. Finally, he managed to reach the monster's tongue, and grabbed onto it with more force than he possibly thought he could muster. The beast thrashed violently; Henry cringed at the horrid vibrations of the beast apparently smashing itself into buildings to try to jar Henry loose. It nearly succeeded. However, driven by the most primal of survival instincts, Henry wrenched himself from the beast's throat and, on wobbly knees, stood hunched in its mouth. With a scream that rose from the very bottom of his gullet, Henry punched upwards with all his strength at the roof of the creature's mouth, foul blood washing over him as he felt flesh sunder. Henry was engulfed in light as the creature's jaws opened, and he hurled himself out, back into the world.

Gasping and shivering as he hit the ground, Henry watched the monster flail around frantically, wantonly destroying anything and everything in its path. Clearly in pain, it was blindly lashing out at its surroundings, and as it transformed edifices into rubble before Henry's eyes, he knew more than ever that he had to stop it. More importantly, he knew that he *could* stop it. Though he was immensely shaken up from nearly being swallowed, the fact that he had survived gave him confidence. Nonetheless, he wanted to wrap this up as quickly as possible.

To attract the creature's attention, he threw the only thing he had near him: a dented traffic cone. It bounced off the beast's face, and the monster responded by charging at Henry. Henry was a bit faster, though, and ran ahead, leading the creature to a construction site nearby. He crashed though the chain link fence, knocking off a sign with the King Industries logo and a diagram of what the site was projected to look like once construction was complete. The creature followed shortly thereafter, obliterating what remained of the fence.

Henry dodged around the side of the skeletal frame of the building under construction and the beast snaked around behind him, bending girders as it barreled through. Henry sprinted to the huge crane next to the building, snagged on to the boom to slow himself down, and swung up to the cab. He opened the door and looked around at the control panel and, seeing two levers, he pulled one of them in hopes of lowering the crane. Nothing. He pushed and pulled on both of them, but the crane was turned off, and they weren't going to work. As Henry fiddled with them, the creature slammed its head against the cab door.

"Damn it," Henry said under his breath as he shoved himself out of the other door. He studied the spool of cable attached to the crane's hook for a moment before kicking it really hard. The cable loosened and, with a harsh metallic whistle, the hook plummeted to the ground.

Vaulting over the cab, Henry accidentally smacked into the left side of the creature's head as he tried to clear it. It twisted its head and snapped at him, trying to devour him once more. Henry rolled to his right and narrowly dodged the jaws, then hopped up and ran over to the hook. He grabbed the cable a few feet from the hook and started to swing it over his head in a circle like a makeshift lasso. The creature turned to face him and raised its head high, watching Henry swing the hook. A thick strand of blood hung off its jaw, dribbling to the ground in oily blobs.

"Come on," said Henry. "Come on!"

Like a toothy tidal wave, the monster charged at Henry, its mouth wide open. Just before it reached Henry, he swung the heavy hook at the side of the creature's head. A sound like a mammoth vase dropping to the floor and shattering reverberated in Henry's ears as the creature's head snapped to the side. But slowly it rose and struck again. This attempt was much more sluggish, and allowed Henry plenty of time to get in one more solid blow with the hook. At this, the creature shuddered, swayed, and finally crashed to the ground, its head falling into a pile of lumber that splintered beneath the weight of the beast's skull. A huge cloud of dust rose, and as bits of debris settled to the ground, Henry dropped the hook and fell to his knees. Save for a few light cracking and rustling noises, the area was silent. Henry placed his palms on the ground and waited for the adrenaline rush to subside.

The sound of voices caused Henry to jump up. Through the dust, he saw two people approaching, one of whom was a woman he recognized from the local news; the other was holding a video camera. The woman was frantically directing the cameraman, who in turn was running around filming the property destruction from all angles, as well as the gargantuan form of the fallen creature. She noticed Henry and pointed at him, motioning the cameraman to follow her as she clambered over debris in high heels.

"Excuse me," she said, "Hi, Helen Slater, Channel 6 news. Did you see what happened here?"

"Yeah," said Henry. "I had a pretty good view of it."

"Well, what was it?" said Helen, motioning to the monster. "What happened to this...thing?"

Henry shrugged. "I beat him up."

"Pardon me?"

"I beat him up," said Henry. "He was demolishing a pretty big chunk of downtown, so I stopped him."

"Um, sure," Helen said. She turned to her camera man, "Is there anyone else around that might have seen what happened?"

Sighing, Henry said, "Fine. Whatever. Can't say I'm surprised you don't believe me. But if you could do me a favor and get out of my way, that'd be great." He picked up the cable lying at his feet. "I don't know if this thing's still alive or not, but if it is, I've got to tie it down before it wakes up."

As Henry went to work wrapping the cable around the creature, the camera man set up a shot where Helen was standing directly in front of the creature.

"Can we get him out of the shot, do you think?" said the camera man, motioning at Henry with his thumb.

"Eh, leave him," said Helen. "As long as we get that big bastard."

One quick call later, and Helen was broadcasting live from the construction site, detailing what little was known about the catastrophe while Henry labored in the background, largely obscured by the wafting haze of dirt and concrete particles. Helen briefly acknowledged him as "an unknown witness," but for the most part focused her commentary on the immense property damage and bizarre, unidentified taxonomy of the creature.

Helen's broadcast was interrupted by the whirring racket of helicopter blades. As she tried to apologize to the station and viewers at home, her words were drowned out to the point where her broadcast had to be temporarily cut off. As the camera man informed her of this, she cursed and glared at the three helicopters landing among the rubble.

Four men jumped out of each helicopter. Most of them looked like SWAT team members, armed men in dark uniforms and sunglasses. Then there were two men in black suits; one of them was a blonde man who looked to be in his late twenties, while the other was a dark haired man with a mustache and clipboard who looked at least twice as old as his compatriot.

"Hurry up," barked the blonde man to the pseudo-SWAT team. "Let's get it contained."

"Ma'am, we're going to have to ask you to leave the area," said one of the armed men to Helen. He then turned to the camera man. "You too. And I'm going to have to confiscate that camera."

"If you're trying to keep this quiet, you're too late," said Helen. "We've already broadcast live. Thousands of people have seen this footage already. So you may as well let us keep the camera. I don't think you'd enjoy the lawsuit that will result if you take it."

The armed man stared at them, then walked back over to

the blonde man. The blonde man barked something and then walked over to Helen, his features contorted into a tight, forced smile.

"Ma'am," he said, extending his hand. "Hi. I understand you're with the local news?"

"Yes," said Helen. "And like I told your friend, we've already broadcast live from this site. So attempting to censor us is really a waste of your time."

"I understand," he said. Without taking his eyes off her, he punched the camera man directly in the jaw, dropping him to the ground. The blonde man then picked up the fallen video camera. "If you want to go ahead with that lawsuit, my name is Tom Tyker. I'm with the United States government, and it would be my pleasure to assist you in seeing that justice is served."

"Hey," said Helen, grabbing at the camera.

Tyker headbutted her, and she crumpled like a paper cup. He then adjusted his tie, and strode back to the dark haired man's side.

"Little rough with them, weren't you, Tom?" said the dark

haired man.

"Eh," said Tyker. "I don't really have time to be arguing with simpletons. So what's the status?"

"It seems to still be alive," said the dark haired man, motioning to the fallen creature that was currently being flanked by the armed men. It lay on the ground, bound with a steel cable by a now-absent Henry Garrison. "And we should have enough tranquilizer to keep it down until we get it back to the facility."

"Should have enough," said Tyker, "or *do* have enough? There's a world of difference there, James."

"Do," said James, his eyes running up and down the text on his clipboard. He scratched something out with a gold ballpoint pen. "That is, as far as I can tell. Anyway, the truck should be here any minute, then we can hightail it."

"What about the guy?"

"What guy? The cameraman?"

"No," said Tyker. "The guy who wrapped this thing up in steel cables. The guy that, as far as we know, single-handedly brought this thing down. That guy."

"Oh. Him," said James. "We'll find him soon enough, I'm sure." He patted the camera. "How many people could there be in this town, anyway?"

"I don't know. But I bet a good chunk of them saw some of this on TV. What are we going to do about that?"

"Let it go, I suppose," said James. "They won't have any real solid evidence of what happened. For all anyone knows, it was a publicity stunt gone awry, a movie being filmed, something like that. Maybe even terrorists. It'll blow over."

"We'd better hope so. The last thing we need is mass hysteria."

"Mass hysteria. That's always a good explanation for things like this," said James, scratching his chin. "You know, I hate all these things, satellite feeds and cell phones and the internet and all that. Everything just happens too quickly. In my day, we actually had some time to operate before information became public."

"In your day," said Tyker, motioning at the creature, "things like that still roamed the Earth freely."

Henry leaned against the wall in an alleyway about a quarter of a mile from where the beast was being loaded into a truck and carted off. He had finished wrapping the cable around the creature just as the helicopters were landing, and decided that he had no desire to deal with whatever sort of people were emerging from them. Grim men with automatic weapons did not figure to give Henry the sort of attention he wanted. His hands on his knees, he tried to catch his breath and process what exactly had just occurred. Was this what it felt like to go insane?

A piece of newspaper, caught in the breeze, brushed up against Henry and he flinched. His insides felt cold, and he was sweating. A narrow shaft of light shone upon his face as the rest of his body was draped in the shadows of the alley. He felt an urge to bite his fingernails, but didn't want to take the gloves off.

"Hey," said a tiny voice behind him, practically causing Henry's skeleton to leap up and liberate itself from his skin. He whirled around, wide-eyed, as he staggered a step back. A sigh of relief swept past his lips as he saw that the source of the voice was a young boy, perhaps 10 years old at the most. He had sparkling blue eyes even wider than Henry's, and was looking up at him with his towhead tilted to one side.

"Yeah?" wheezed Henry. "What can I do for ya?"

"Um," said the little boy, choosing his words carefully, "you're the man who...the one who fought the monster, right?"

"What monster?" said Henry.

"The big one. The snake," said the boy. "I saw it."

"What were you doing around there? That was dangerous. Why didn't you run away?"

"It was cool. I've never seen a monster before."

"Yeah. Well, let's hope you never see one again," said Henry. "You should probably get home."

"Can I ask you a question?"

Henry stared at the boy. He was unsure whether this was a positive development or not. "Yeah. Sure."

"Why aren't you more hurt?"

"Excuse me?"

"You're not bleeding. I don't see any bruises. Your jacket isn't even ripped."

Henry gave himself a quick once over. The kid was right. At least he wasn't going to have to spend eighteen more dollars getting another sweatshirt monogrammed. His unusual durability didn't really make a lot of sense, but neither did anything else about this afternoon.

"I don't know," Henry said. "I wish I could tell you, but I don't know myself."

"I recorded it," said the kid, fishing a cell phone out of his pocket. "On this."

"Recorded what?"

"You. Fighting the monster. I mean, I didn't get all of it, but I got some."

"Can I see it?"

The boy hesitated, and cupped his hands over the phone, pulling it to his chest. "You're not gonna take it from me, are you?"

"No," said Henry. "I wouldn't do that."

The boy stared at Henry for a few moments, then held out the cell phone in front of him. "Check it out," he said.

The two of them watched the pixilated but unmistakable

video of Henry slugging it out with the enormous serpent. The footage was shaky, and ended before the fight transferred to the construction site, but it was still compelling. Henry felt a swell of pride as he watched himself do battle with the creature. "That's pretty cool," he said. "Can I have a copy of that?"

"This is a phone," said the boy. "How can I give you a copy of it?"

"Can't you upload it to your computer and e-mail it or something?"

"I don't know how to do that."

"...Right," said Henry. "Sorry. What are you gonna do with it, then?"

"I don't know, show it to my friends."

"Well, have fun," said Henry. "Just don't lose that video, OK?"

"Oh, I won't."

Henry turned around, figuring he should probably get home. "Hey," said the boy, causing him to turn around once more.

"Yeah?"

"What's your name?"

"Henry Garrison," said Henry, smiling. "If you need a reminder, check out the back of my sweatshirt."

"Oh, yeah," said the boy, craning his neck to get a better look at the lettering on Henry's back. "Cool!"

"Take care, man," said Henry. Then he leapt up onto the roof to go reclaim his belongings. His parents were probably worried about him and he needed to get home.

Chapter Six

Henry had barely set foot in his house before finding himself wrapped in his mother's Palmolive-scented embrace.

"Oh my God, Henry," she said, her voice quivering, "I was so worried. I heard about something terrible going on downtown, and you were late getting home, and I just thought that maybe you..."

"I'm fine, mom," Henry said, patting his mother's back. "Honestly. I'm OK. See?"

"Of course. Of course," she said, pulling back and wiping some condensation from the corner of her eye. "I'm just really happy to see you."

"So you're alright, then?" his father said from the couch. "That's a relief. Did you happen to see what was going on out there?"

"Huh? Oh, no," said Henry slowly. "You know. Detention

and everything. I wouldn't know if a bomb went off. I didn't see anything weird on the way home, so…"

"Well, I guess something happened downtown," said his father, grabbing the remote control from the coffee table. "I don't know what it was. Terrorists or something, maybe. I don't know why they would be attacking here, but it must have been pretty bad. Our phones have been out and the TV hasn't been working."

Henry turned to view the hissing fuzz on the television and wondered if Helen Slater's broadcast from the construction site had even made it on to television and, if so, how many people had actually been able to watch it. It had never occurred to him that the creature's path of destruction might have disrupted communications throughout St. Dante; then again, life or death battles with enormous monsters tend to consume most of one's active thought process. Though he felt some sense of relief due to the fact that he didn't have to explain his super powered brawl to his parents, he felt some disappointment regarding the possibility that no one may have seen anything about him on television. He sighed heavily. "Well," he said, "I'm glad to know that I avoided whatever went on. It sounds pretty bad."

"Yeah," his father said with a snort. "I considered going down to check it out, but since I don't really know the nature of what's happening, I figured, why take the risk?"

"Good idea," said Henry. "We should probably stay inside for now, until we know what's up…just to be on the safe side."

The telephone rang. "There's a good sign," said Henry's mother. "At least something's working." She walked over to the phone and picked up the receiver.

"It's a hell of a thing," said Henry's father. "I hope no one we know was hurt…I just really wish I knew what was happening."

"What?" said Henry's mother from the kitchen. "You're kidding me!"

"Well, hey," said Henry, "If ever there was a good day to not have a job, right?"

"Yeah," said Henry's father with a slight chuckle. "If ever."

"Turn on the TV," said Henry's mother, her right hand covering the phone.

"It's working now?" said Henry's father.

"It should be. Turn it on; Patti says they're showing some video about the attack downtown."

Henry's eyebrows lowered as his father picked up the remote control and clicked the television on. He tensed up; he had no idea what might greet them when the television picture faded in, nor what the resulting reaction might be. The suspense was suffocating.

The image of stoic, grandfatherly local newsman Edward Beaumont emerged from the television's shiny blackness. He was hunched over his desk and staring in a way that made it seem as though he was making direct eye contact with the viewer no matter where they might be situated in the room. His phlegmy baritone rumbled forth; he was mid-sentence.

"-vary as to the exact nature of the disturbance, Channel 5 has procured a video that is reputed to show exactly what occurred in St. Dante. It is not the highest quality, but what it shows is both shocking and unmistakable. I warn you: the footage is, to say the least, unbelievable."

The heavily distorted image of a young man in a black

sweatshirt doing battle with an immense serpent filled the screen. A brown, dusty haze blanketed the scene, and made the already pixilated images even more abstract, like Jerry Bruckheimer had commissioned a Monet painting, but the action was still unmistakable. Henry winced as he watched the creature smash him through windows, and felt a flush of pride as he relived himself belting the monster right in the face. Nonetheless, he thought, this shouldn't be happening. This shouldn't be on television. How…?

"That little liar," Henry said under his breath.

"Though the identity of the individual in this footage is unclear due to its low quality, it seems to be legitimate," said the reporter. "The original source of the footage is a cell phone, sent over to the station by a viewer. Channel 5 News has extracted the video straight from the source, and so far it is the only evidence we have of what occurred this afternoon. Authorities are looking for any information that might lead them to the identity of the individual in the video, as well as the whereabouts of the creature responsible for the destruction. There are, naturally, a great deal of unanswered questions regarding this situation."

Henry couldn't help but blush as his parents stared at him.

"That was you," said his mother, pointing.

"Yeah…I know," said Henry.

"You were fighting that…thing?" said Henry's father.

"Uh, yes," said Henry. "I was. Maybe now, when I tell you something, you'll listen to me. Like, say, when I sit you down to tell you that I have superpowers."

"But…how? I don't understand," said his mother.

"Yeah, well, neither do I. Nor do I understand why a huge monster would all of a sudden appear and start smashing the town to bits. But it is what it is."

"I need to lie down," said Henry's mother, and she headed upstairs.

"Do you think maybe you could wash my sweatshirt for me at some point tonight? It's disgusting," he called after her. After a few moments of silence, he mumbled, "Never mind. I'll do it myself."

"So…wow. Really," said Henry's father. "So this isn't some kind of joke or something?"

"As much as I would like to take the credit for being able to plan out such an elaborate hoax," said Henry, sitting down on the couch, "that would be a no. This is real. And I don't have any idea what to do about it."

"What do you mean?"

"Well, it's like, I have these abilities-and believe me, I'm thrilled about that-but I don't really know if there's any practical application for them. For whatever reason, people always think whatever I do is some kind of trick. For example, I lifted up a statue in the park the other day hoping it would get me on the news, but people swore they could see the strings holding it up."

"There was an episode of *Twilight Zone* like that."

"I know, right? That's what I was saying."

"Well, I mean, you got on the news today, right? So you got what you wanted."

"Yeah, I guess. But now I have no clue what's going on. There's a monster running around and God knows where it even came from and I somehow manage to take it out and then a bunch of guys come in helicopters and stuff to deal with it..."

"Wait, what?"

"Exactly. It's insane. So now I'm just kind of hoping the whole thing goes away. I just…I don't know, I can't shake the feeling that somehow this is my fault. The fact that I would randomly get superpowers, followed immediately by the appearance of some monster that shouldn't even exist…it's just too much of a coincidence, and I'm kind of thinking that I don't want any part of it."

"Well, let's not go crazy here. I mean, with abilities like yours, you could be rich. *We* could be rich," his father said. "What can you do, exactly, anyway? Can you fly?"

"No, can't fly," said Henry. "But I'm really, really strong. And fast. So that's something."

"It'd be really neat if you could fly."

"Yes, OK, wonderful. I'll file a complaint to whoever's in charge of these things."

"Huh?"

"Never mind. I'm going to take a shower, I feel like rooster vomit."

Henry exited the bathroom in a black t-shirt and red flannel boxer shorts, wiping away the trickling annoyance of an errant drop of water running down his forehead. After precisely one and a half steps, his father called up to him.

"Henry, the sheriff's here to see you," he said.

"Damn it," Henry grumbled, an icy pang of fear jabbing petulantly at his heart. "I'll be right down. Just let me put some pants on."

"That'd be very kind of you," the sheriff said.

"Are you taking me to the station or something?" said Henry, now with pants on, a few minutes later.

"No, no," said the sheriff. "I just wanted to talk to you about something. We can do that here, if you've got some place we can sit down."

"Oh. Yeah, sure," said Henry. "My room's probably out, but there's a study over here that we never use for anything. If that's alright with you."

"Sounds fine."

Henry, heart palpitations and all, led the sheriff into the study and sat him at an old cherry wood table. It had likely once been very nice, but years of scuffs and scratches and coaster-less beverages had left it worn, if still vaguely handsome. The same description could be applied to the sheriff, who had introduced himself as Porter during a brief, firm handshake. He had thinning white hair and a bushy mustache, and his skin was beginning to bunch up like a bathroom rug. He was tall and lean and, despite his weathered exterior, projected an air of tired forcefulness. His blue eyes were keen, and his mouth had a slight pout that belied no emotion at all. He smelled like soap and tobacco.

"Do you want some water or something?" Henry said, settling down in his chair.

"No, no. I'm fine," said Porter. "This shouldn't take too long."

Henry squirmed in his seat and stared at the sheriff. Porter stared back for a moment, then looked away and said with a sigh, "So I'm sure you are aware that there was a…very large disturbance downtown this afternoon."

"Yes sir."

"A very unusual and highly destructive disturbance."

"Yes sir."

"Well," said Porter, "You're probably also aware that, aside from the numerous unbelievable eyewitness accounts, there is a grainy but very informative video of the incident as well."

"Yeah," Henry said, his voice quivering a bit, "I, uh, I saw some of it."

"We got a couple of calls down at the station," Porter said slowly, leaning in, "and it seems that, according to the aforementioned tipsters, you in particular appear to be the individual…the *human* individual in question, on this video tape."

Henry was sweating. The sheer length of the sheriff's sentences was making him nervous.

"Can you confirm that this is indeed the case?"

Henry took a deep breath. "Yes," he said, staring down at the table. "That would be the case."

"Alright," Porter said, leaning back in his chair. "Good. Ok. So now the question is, exactly what the hell was going on this afternoon that left a sizable section of my town in ruins?"

"Um, well, a big snake monster thing came out of God knows where, and I managed to stop its, um, destructive rampage. Unfortunately, that's the best explanation I have for you at this point in time."

Porter sighed and folded his hands across his stomach. "You understand, of course, that there are certain issues I might have with that explanation you've just given me. Not the least of which is the fact that the, urm, 'big snake monster' is absolutely nowhere to be found. Even given the sudden nature of its appearance, I am having some difficulty explaining just how a...creature of that magnitude simply up and vanishes."

"Well that I can help you with," said Henry. "Pretty much right after I took it down, some helicopters showed up, and a bunch of guys came out. Some were...I don't know, soldiers or something, and there were a couple of guys in suits."

"Suits? What sort of suits?"

"I don't know. Nice suits."

"Yes, OK, but what I mean is, were they hazmat suits?

Jumpsuits?"

"No," said Henry. "Just dress-up suits. Like Armani or something, whatever. They looked very official."

"What do you mean, official?"

"I guess, like, you know, official. Like FBI agents on TV. Sunglasses and all that."

"Did you speak to these men? Did they speak to you?"

"No," said Henry. "I don't know…I didn't really like the vibe they were giving off. There was all this commotion and I didn't want to be involved. I guess I panicked; I just didn't want to be involved in all that. It was too weird for me."

"Of course you do understand," said Porter, scratching his forehead, "that when you engaged that creature you were already involved."

"With that, yeah," said Henry. "But whoever these guys were that came afterwards, I didn't want anything to do with them."

"So you don't know what they did with the creature?"

"Nope. Couldn't tell ya. I didn't stick around that long."

"And I suppose you don't know where it came from in the

first place, then."

"Absolutely no idea. I was in detention. You can ask the principal."

Porter clasped his hands together, as if in prayer, and rubbed them over his nose. "Alright. Well, one more thing then," he said. "How on God's green Earth were you able to put down an enormous snake-like monster with your bare hands? Is there any possible way you can explain that to me so that it makes sense?"

"Oh yeah," said Henry, smirking. "That's easy. I have superpowers."

"Superpowers."

"Yes. I'm super strong, super fast, just super all-around. It's a recent development, but rest assured, you'll be hearing more about it."

"And you expect me to believe this," said Porter.

"Actually, no. Not really. I'm finding that, for whatever reason, no one really believes me, so I wouldn't expect you too, either. But I'm prepared to show you if you'd like to see."

"No, that'll be fine," said Porter, rising from his seat.

"Another time, perhaps."

"I'm just saying, it's really cool," said Henry. "I could lift your car up or something."

"I'll be in touch, Henry," Porter said, extending his hand. "Just do me a favor and don't leave town anytime soon, OK?"

"Wouldn't dream of it," said Henry, grasping Porter's hand and shaking it vigorously.

Porter walked to the front door, nodding at Henry's father as he departed.

"You'll believe me," Henry called after him. "Just wait."

"I'm sure I will," said Porter, who glanced quickly at Henry with baleful eyes. "You have a good night."

As the front door shut, Henry sat down on the couch. This was not good; whatever heinous chicanery the sheriff thought Henry might be up to, their conversation had clearly not done anything to allay his suspicions. And the fact that Porter seemingly had no clue who the men in suits were, or even that they existed at all, was worrisome. He would have to figure out how best to handle this.

Henry's father walked over and sat down next to him, putting his hand on Henry's shoulder. "Henry?" he said.

"Yeah?"

"Would you mind showing me the thing where you lift up the statue?"

Henry plunked himself down in his bed and stared at the ceiling. His eyes roved over the little white balls, like cottage cheese, that made up the ceiling's barren canvas. There was some sort of black blot scuttling amongst the balls; probably a spider. Henry scowled and shuddered a bit despite himself, then rolled to his side. The worn leather gloves lay balled up on his nightstand, an innocuous lump. Beside them lay Henry's cell phone. He reached out halfheartedly and squinted at the screen. Eight missed calls, and at least one message. He pushed a button and heard a brief, spirited jingle to indicate that the phone was shutting off. Setting the phone down, Henry glanced up at the black blot once more. It was scuttling away, destination unknown. With a slight groan, Henry rolled onto his stomach and closed his eyes. He fell asleep with the lights still on.

Henry's cell phone was still turned off when he arrived at school the next day. The walk from his home, which normally took about twelve minutes, took almost twenty today. He continuously, unthinkingly balled and unballed his fists the entire way. As he stepped through the heavy iron gates that marked the entrance to St. Dante High, he scanned the students milling about. There was a good deal more turmoil than usual, with students babbling excitedly about the previous day's destruction downtown. Tucking his thumb underneath his backpack straps, Henry headed in, his eyes darting from side to side. He accidentally swung his lunchbox into the backside of a girl who glared at him, but other than that, no one really seemed to note his presence any more than usual. Perhaps his anxiety regarding the repercussions of yesterday's incident had been unfounded.

A pair of boys that Henry was vaguely familiar with stepped out in front of him.

"Hey," said the first boy, a blonde kid wearing a black jacket with a single red stripe across it, "are you that guy?"

"What guy?" said Henry, looking over the boy's shoulder.

"The guy from the news. From yesterday," said the boy, wagging his finger at Henry.

"Yeah! Yeah, that *is* the guy!" said the other boy. He was a short fellow with a Yankees cap and a yellow t-shirt covered in indecipherable scrawls.

"What are you talking about?" Henry muttered. Maybe he should have worn a different sweatshirt.

"You're the guy from the news," the blonde boy said. "You were fighting some animal or something downtown yesterday, right? I saw the video."

"In that case," said Henry with a slight chuckle, "yeah, I guess that was me, then."

"Holy crap," said the kid in the Yankees cap. "What happened? What did you do?" A small, murmuring crowd was beginning to form around the boys.

"It's sort of hard to explain," Henry said, scratching his right eyebrow. "I wasn't…well, I mean, I wasn't expecting it. It just sort of happened."

"Yeah, but *what* happened?"

"Not much to it, really," said Henry with a shrug. "There was some…I guess, animal that was rampaging around downtown. Big thing, ugly. Somebody had to do something, obviously, and so I took care of it."

"How, though?"

"Well, if you really want to know," Henry said with a grin, "I took it down with my bare hands."

"Bull*crap*," said the blonde boy. "Get out of here. There's no way."

"Suit yourself. You're the one who asked," said Henry. "I'm just telling you what happened."

"OK, fine then," said the boy with the Yankees cap. "How did you take it down then? Did you make like some kind of a trap or something?" The crowd of students observing the exchange was steadily growing and yet increasingly quiet.

"Not at all," said Henry. "It wasn't really necessary. I mean, I can punch a hole through a brick wall. What the hell do I need a trap for?"

"What are you talking about?"

"Did you not hear me?" Henry said. His eyebrows were arched and his voice was steadily rising. He was gesturing in an exaggerated manner, and his lunchbox was flopping around on its handle. "I can punch a hole through a brick wall. I can lift a statue over my head. I can…I don't know, do things requiring a lot of strength…I probably could have ended that sentence stronger."

"Yeah, sure," said the blonde boy. "What, are you Superman or something?"

"Something like that," said Henry, staring him straight in the eye, unblinking. Then he snapped his head back and laughed. "Look, I'm whatever. Believe me or don't. I certainly don't expect you to. I'm just answering your question. That's all." He turned to walk away.

"Hold on," said a voice behind Henry. He whirled around to see Doug standing there.

"Oh, hey," said Henry. "Morning."

Trent and Albert emerged from the crowd and stood beside

Doug. Doug shoved his hands into his pockets and kicked at a pebble on the ground. "If you can lift up a car," he said, "prove it. I'd like to see that."

"Well, I-" said Henry. As he spoke, the second period bell rang. Considering the principal's opinion of him, it seemed an unwise move to encourage truancy among a group of students. Looking up into the gray, unsettled morning sky, he said, "Come back here during lunch. All of you. I'll prove to you what I can do, if you really want to know." Then he turned, and walked off to class. He felt his face tightening up, and wasn't completely certain whether it was due to a smile or a wince.

"Well, this ought to be something," said Trent during the day's morning break. A faint drizzle had started to blanket the campus, and the four friends were sitting in their usual spot, staying dry under the awning. Owing to the weather, there were significantly more people up on the wood shop walkway than usual today. Many of them stared at Henry and whispered amongst themselves.

"What are you going to do?" asked Albert. Henry didn't respond. He leaned on the worn, orange railing and stared out across the depopulated court as raindrops tapdanced upon every uncovered surface.

"He's not listening," said Doug, flipping through the pages of his binder. "What I'm wondering is what he can do that can possibly top what he did yesterday."

"Nothing," mumbled Henry. "But that doesn't matter. No one saw what I did yesterday."

"What are you talking about?" said Trent. "Just about everybody saw it. On TV, anyway."

"Yeah, but you heard those guys this morning," said Henry, turning around and leaning his back up against the railing. "They don't believe that for a second. And I don't blame them. I mean, most of the crap you see on TV is phony anyway. Even the stuff that's ostensibly real. Why should I be any different?"

"Because you *are* different," said Albert. "I wasn't there yesterday, but I know that what they showed on the news happened. Just look at downtown, for God's sake. It's a disaster area."

"Hey, what happened with that, anyway?" said Doug. "That thing, the monster or whatever. Where did it go? Did you disintegrate it or something?"

"That would be awesome! But no, I don't even know where it went," Henry sighed. "Believe me, if I did, I'd have told the sheriff last night. It's not easy to prove something that's completely unbelievable when the biggest piece of evidence has gone missing. Anyway, all I know is that some guys showed up and took it somewhere. Soldiers and guys in suits."

"Oooh, how *X-Files*," said Trent.

"What a timely reference," said Doug.

"Eat me," said Trent.

"Tell me about it," said Henry, blithely ignoring the banter. "But yeah, no idea what happened there, really."

"Weird," said Trent.

"Spooky," said Albert.

"Etcetera," said Doug.

"So as I said, I can't really upstage my little skirmish

yesterday. But that's unnecessary," said Henry. "All I'm going to do is a simple feat of strength, to prove that what I said is true."

"But you tried that already," said Doug. "In the park, with the statue. You may recall that that incident did not go particularly well. You actually failed to prove anything, and everyone who saw you thought you were pulling some trick."

"Yes, I do recall," said Henry. "But at that point, I was just some random guy. Now I have a little bit more notoriety. I've already made a case for myself with the news broadcast. Now I just have to prove it."

"I see," said Doug. "So you think it's gonna work this time?"

"I don't know. Maybe," said Henry. "One thing I'm sure of: this time, I let *them* choose what I lift up."

"Ah, a man of the people," said Doug.

When Henry arrived at the gates of the school seven minutes after the lunch bell rang, flanked by Doug, Albert and Trent, a small crowd had begun to gather. Murmurs mixed with the hissing of falling rain as many sets of expectant eyes rose from beneath hoods, caps, and umbrellas.

"Ladies, gentlemen," said Henry. "Thanks for coming out. I promise you it'll be worth getting soaked."

"It better be," someone said.

"So what we're going to do here," said Doug, stepping out in front of Henry, "is quite simple. My friend here has been the subject of some debate lately, and he is going to prove to you all today, definitively, that he is capable of extraordinary things."

"Thank you," said Henry.

"What debate?" said the boy with the Yankees cap from this morning. "I haven't heard any debate."

"What? You *started* the debate," said Henry.

"I did not."

"Anyway," Doug said, "We're going to display to you today, before your very eyes, that my friend Henry Garrison is capable of amazing things; superhuman things! Now I understand that this may be difficult for you to believe, and we don't expect you to just take our word for it. So the proposition that I make to you is-"

"Tell me something to lift, and I'll lift it," Henry interjected.

"Yes," said Doug.

"Like what?" said the blonde boy from this morning. He blinked as water dripped from his hair into his eyes.

"Like, I don't know, something really heavy. Whatever."

"Lift up the whole school," said the boy with the Yankees cap.

"What?"

"Yeah," said the blonde boy. "Do that. Lift up the whole school.'

"Now how am I supposed to do that?" said Henry.

"I don't know. You're the superman."

"That's a stupid idea."

"Whatever," said the boy with the Yankees cap. "I think it's a great idea."

"I do too," said the blonde boy.

"Thank you," said the boy in the Yankees cap.

"God," said Trent.

"OK, look, can someone give me a reasonable suggestion

here?" said Henry, shaking his head.

"Why don't you lift up my car," said a syrupy voice from within the crowd. Immediately following the proclamation, its source emerged from the crowd. Roderick King III stood before Henry wearing a peacoat and a sneer. "I'd be pretty impressed if you could do that."

"I think that's a great idea, Rod," said Henry. "But are you sure you'd trust me with your car? I might throw it off a cliff or something."

"Of course I'd trust you," said Roderick. "Because if you damage it, every penny's worth of repairs is coming out of your pocket. And I know damn well your family can't afford that. Is your father even working yet?"

"Fine. Your car it is," said Henry. He turned to his friends. "Come on," he said with a snort, and strode off through the veil of precipitation. Albert and Trent silently followed.

"Come on, folks," said Doug to the crowd. "Let's go to the parking lot."

The crowd picked up some more members as several

students, curious about exactly what was going on, assimilated into the mass of people as it passed by them. Henry walked briskly ahead, his eyes downcast, watching water droplets roll off his gloves. He rubbed his hands together, and was jolted to sudden feel the rain peppering his skin. Water began to seep through the canvas parts of his shoes, stowing away in the tiny rivet holes on the sides. The onset of soggification in his socks made him walk all the faster.

"Which one is your car?" Henry yelled back at Roderick once the group reached the parking lot.

Roderick pointed at a beautiful black Mercedes Benz. "Think you can lift that?"

"No problem," said Henry. He held up his gloved hands. "See? I won't even get fingerprints on it."

Henry hunched down and peered closely at the Benz. He had never even contemplated lifting a car over his head before, and had no idea how to actually go about it. Should he grip the bumper? Maybe he should open the door and lift it by the roof…no, but then he would probably have to hold it upside down. Should he get under the car? Finally, he crouched and put his hands underneath the car, beneath the passenger side door, midway between the wheels. He shuffled forward on his haunches until his arms were beneath the car up to the elbow.

OK, he thought. Here we go. Lift with your legs, not your arms. Just because you have super strength doesn't mean you should risk throwing your back out. Don't screw this up.

Steadying himself, Henry blew some air through pursed lips with a barely audible whistle, whispered, "Here we go," and stood up gingerly, raising the car up to chest level. As he adjusted his hold on it so that he could lift it over his head, the car alarm went off. Loud whoops and sirens tore through the moist air. Despite the fiercely annoying din, the crowd of students stood slack-jawed, transfixed by the awesome display of strength before them. Even Roderick was held speechless. As Henry gave him a smug grin, he noticed Denise Hargrove standing next to Roderick.

"See, Denise?" Henry yelled over the alarm's awful screeching. "Now you know how I hit that home run the other day."

"Wait, you're the guy who hit the home run?" asked the boy

with the Yankees cap. "I heard about that. That was supposed to be really something."

"Yep, that was me," said Henry with a chuckle, idly spinning the car over his head. "All me."

"Aren't you also the guy who got peed on in P.E.?" said the blonde boy.

"Oh yeah, somebody peed on him, huh?" said the boy with the Yankess cap.

"Actually," said Doug, "that's inaccurate. He did not get peed on. What happened was, he happened to put a P.E. uniform on that had been soaking in a urine-filled toilet without his knowledge."

"No further questions," said Henry, setting down the Benz. "Jeez, Rod…you think you could turn off on this alarm? It's driving me nuts."

"Nope. Sorry," said Roderick. "Can't do it."

"Why the hell not? Is the sound of irritating wailing music to your ears?"

"No, not at all," said Roderick, crossing his arms. "But

there's nothing I can do about it. That's not even my car."

"Excuse me?" said Henry. "Then who the hell's car is it?"

"Him," said Roderick, pointing behind Henry.

Henry turned around to find himself inches away from Mr. Sadek's scowling visage. A raindrop hung from his noise like a liquefied stalactite, and his angry mutterings floated away on steam clouds.

"Aw, damn it," said Henry.

"I had to ban you from P.E.," Mr. Sadek said glumly. "Now do I have to ban you from the parking lot, too? You know, I could have you arrested for vandalism after that little stunt you just pulled."

"I am *so* sorry," said Henry, slumped in the chair. "I told you, I didn't know that was your car."

"And that's supposed to make it OK?" said Mr. Sadek. "Look, I don't know what is going on lately, but if you think your shenanigans are appropriate, you've got another thing coming. After what happened yesterday, people are scared and confused. The last thing you should be doing is causing more chaos around here."

"Hey, look," said Henry, sitting straight up, "I was right in the middle of that thing yesterday, and believe me, I'm just as confused as anybody. Now I don't know if you saw the news yesterday, but-"

"I saw the news," said Mr. Sadek. "I saw it, but you know what? I don't know what I saw. Between that and seeing you lift a car over your head, and you hurting that boy in P.E. class…well, I really don't know what to think about the whole thing. And frankly, I'm kind of hoping that it just goes away before I have a stroke and die."

"Well, I-"

"Listen," said Mr. Sadek, "I had a couple of men in here this morning who said they were with the government, and they were looking for a student in this school…the boy from the news, they said. Now, Henry, I know that they were here for you, I know it now and I knew it then, but I didn't tell them who you were. God knows why, but I didn't tell them. But if you ask me, you're in some big trouble, and those definitely seem like the sort of men that will find you eventually, with or without my help."

Henry lowered his face into the palms of his hands. "I know who you're talking about," he said. "And thanks for having my back. But you're right, there's not much sense in hiding from them. I mean, damn near everybody in the school knows about me, and with St. Dante being what it is, I would imagine the entire population would know by, what, tomorrow afternoon?"

"Do you know what they want?"

"Probably just to question me," said Henry. "The sheriff already did, so why not? Anyway, I didn't do anything wrong, so I'm not too worried. Unless saving lives is illegal or something."

Mr. Sadek took a sip of coffee. "I just hope for your sake that you didn't have anything to do with all this."

"Of course I had something to do with it," said Henry. "I stopped it. And that's it. Can I go now? I'm going to miss Spanish if I stay in here any longer."

"Yes, fine. Go," said Mr. Sadek. "But don't forget about detention today."

"Wild horses couldn't drag me away," said Henry, pushing

himself out of his seat and heading out the door.

"Just be careful," Mr. Sadek called out from behind him. "One of our students being incarcerated reflects poorly upon the whole school."

As Henry strode out of the office, he failed to notice Roderick, pressed up against the wall just around the corner from the principal's office, watching and listening intently.

The march home from detention was a strange one. Part of Henry expected to hear shrieks and roars and smashing, the soundtrack to another massive crisis. Another part of him expected a cadre of soldiers to leap out of the bushes and swarm him like heavily armed locusts, dragging him away to some secret location for an unspeakably brutal interrogation. Yet another part of him wanted to wrap his arms around the trunk of a tree, yank it from the ground, and see how far he could toss it, just for kicks. And a fourth part just wanted to sleep.

As these warring parts clouded Henry's mind with muddled paranoia, a figure stepped into the road in front of Henry. He immediately recognized the figure as the strange, huge pale man he had seen a few days prior. The man seemed impossibly solid, like a marble sculpture that some mad artist had dressed up and left in the street as a massive curiosity. He was wearing the same black coat and shiny boots he had been in his previous encounter with Henry, but this time the coat was open, revealing an unusual deep purple bodysuit that seemed to be made of some latexy looking material that Henry had never seen before. Purely on instinct, Henry scuttled to the side of the road to edge past the man.

"Hold on," said the man. His voice was coarse and raspy, and had a strange accent to it that Henry couldn't place. It wasn't German, or Russian, but perhaps somewhere in between. It was a harsh accent, verbal sandpaper, with which even the most benign statement would sound like a death threat. That it was coming from this monolithic devil made it all the more imposing.

"Yeah?" said Henry, his voice cracking despite himself. "Can I help you with something?"

"Yes, in fact, you can," said the man, his eyes twinkling. "I am going to need you to come with me."

Chapter Seven

"Excuse me?" said Henry, taking a step back. "Come with you? Where?"

"That would be rather difficult to explain," said the man. His voice was soft, but his peculiar accent made it seem thunderous. "But suffice it to say I need your help."

"Yeah, but for what? Do you have a flat tire or something?"

"A flat…? No," said the man. "But I am being rude. I have not introduced myself. My name is Vargas."

"Henry. Nice to, ah, meet you," said Henry, taking another step backward. There was something about the man that chilled him, something unnatural that made his hands quiver. "Anyway, I really have to get going. I have a lot of things to do, but good luck and…yeah, good luck."

"I am afraid I cannot let you go," said Vargas. He didn't move a muscle, yet Henry felt as though the man was looming over him, a white shadow.

"That's, um, that's really...sweet of you to say," said Henry, squinting and beginning to actively walk away. His knees felt weak, and he would have gladly been whisked away to absolutely anywhere in the world to get away from here. "But I really do have to be on my way." He turned his back to the man and half-jogged away.

Without warning, Henry felt Vargas's hand upon his left shoulder. Reflexively, he turned and swatted the hand away, and hopped backwards a couple of feet. "Hey, man," he said, "don't touch me. I'm serious."

"My apologies," said Vargas with a laugh like a rattlesnake's hiss, "but you are not leaving me much choice. I am quite serious myself. And I am going to need you to come with me."

"Look, I don't know what you want, but no. Not interested," said Henry. He thought of what the principal had told him before, about men in suits coming around looking for him. Could this man have something to do what that? It seemed unlikely, as the man's appearance did not line up with that of well-dressed professionals, but the situation as a whole was bizarre enough that Henry could not completely discount the possibility. "Now really, leave me alone. I don't know who you think I am, but I assure you, I'm not the guy you want to be messing with right now. At all. So…goodbye. Don't touch me, don't follow me."

"You are making this very difficult," said Vargas, stepping toward Henry, "but I suppose you would not be of much use to me if you did not have some fight in you. So in a way, this is a good thing."

"OK, listen," said Henry. "I'm done with you. You're giving me the creeps, and I'm getting out of here. And if you follow me, I'm going to make sure this is a very bad day for you. You're messing with forces you can't possibly understand." He turned and stomped away, smiling just a bit, inwardly. He had always wanted to say that.

Henry shuddered as he felt Vargas grip his left arm. "GET OFF ME!" Henry roared, and swung his right fist at Vargas. In the instant before it connected, Henry filled with dread and regret; he was surely going to put the man in a hospital, or worse. But physics is hard on takebacks, and Henry's fist collided with Vargas's chest.

Vargas staggered backwards, then straightened up. "Hmm," he said. "Not bad. Decent force to it. Good reaction time."

"What the hell?" said Henry. "How are you still standing after that?'

"Do not flatter yourself," Vargas said. "That was alright, but it would take much more than that to do me any real harm."

"I don't understand," said Henry.

"Of course you do not," Vargas said with a rueful sneer. He crossed his arms across his chest. "You do not want me to explain anything. You just want to hit me when I will not go away."

"I'll admit, I'm intrigued," said Henry. "I was about to start rehearsing my plea bargain, and then you go and take a pretty solid punch like it's a stiff breeze. As weird as this week as been, that may have been the capper. So tell me: how?"

"How what?"

"How are you not on your ass right now?"

"Ah. That is fairly simple. I am wearing armor," said Vargas, lightly tapping his fist against his chest. "As you can tell, it is quite effective."

"That doesn't look like any armor I've ever seen," said Henry. "Actually, it looks sort of goofy, like you're in a German metal band or something."

Vargas scowled. "Well of course it does not look like anything you have ever seen," he said. "Your people have nowhere near the level of technology to construct something like this."

"Excuse me?" said Henry. "My people? What's that supposed to mean? White people?"

"I mean the people…of this world," said Vargas, shaking his head. "It is not your fault, but you are well behind us."

"OK, so you're a space alien now," said Henry. "Look, Crazy, I'm leaving. I really don't need any of this right now."

"I never said I was a space alien," said Vargas. "Although in a sense I suppose that might be true. But no, I am not some creature from another planet in your galaxy, if that is what you mean. I am not actually from this plane of existence at all. I am, for lack of a better term, from another…dimension."

"Another dimension," said Henry, his left eyebrow raised.

"Like Dimension X?"

"I am sorry?"

"*Ninja Turtles*? It's the dimension the bad guys are from? No? Never mind," said Henry. "Look, I really don't have the time or energy for this right now. Let's say, for the sake of argument, that you are from another dimension. One, why should I believe you, and two, what does any of this have to do with me?"

"This has everything to do with you," said Vargas. "You are the reason I am here. I need your help, and you are going to give it to me."

"Is that so?" said Henry. "Listen, I don't care what kind of armor you have or how deep your voice is. I don't know what your deal is, but I don't take orders very well, especially from lunatics who think they're from another dimension. Best of luck." He turned to walk away. Just as quickly as he turned, Vargas was right in front of him.

"My patience is at an end," Vargas said. "I will not argue with you anymore. You will come with me now." He reached out a huge hand.

Henry leapt backwards with a shout. "I told you not to touch me."

Vargas was instantly upon him, a darting shroud. "Do be quiet," he said, punching Henry in the stomach. To Henry's shock, the force of the blow was massive, a compact battering ram that sent him to his knees filled with searing numbness.

Vargas stood above Henry with his arms crossed. "Really, I think you have wasted enough of my time. Now you are coming with me, one way or another. If I have to beat you into quivering jelly, so be it. Just so long as you heal eventually."

Henry grabbed at Vargas's leg, but Vargas kicked his hand away. "What do you want from me?" Henry coughed.

"My world is not like this one," said Vargas. "It is a much darker, more violent place. You have the sun here, blue skies. Where I come from, the sky is ever a shade of purple; any sun we may have had was mostly blotted out long ago. War rages, a ponderous, bloody stalemate with no resolution in sight. I tire of the endless conflict, and so I have decided to tip the scales in favor of my side. I have been combing every country, every planet, every dimension for powerful magical energies in the hopes that I might find someone like you, someone with enough power to turn the tides of war. Lo and behold, here you are. A bit disappointing, I must admit; by the amount of energy radiating from you, I estimated you would be significantly more powerful than you seem to actually be, but I sense enough potential in you that I think I can mold you into a capable warrior. In any case, you would be wise to accompany me without any further struggle; I would hate to accidentally cripple you." Vargas made an uncomfortable attempt to smile.

"Like hell," said Henry as he rose to his feet, his voice and knees quivering in weak, clammy syncopation. "I-I'm not going anywhere with you. You can take your pasty ass back to your alternate dimension and forget about me, because this? Uh-uh. This isn't happening."

"It is really the least you could do," Vargas said. "After all, I have lost my pet because of you. Those things are not easily replaceable. You owe me."

"Wow. And how is that, exactly? Is it my fault your alien

dog ran away from home? Are you ever going to start making sense?"

"Just because you are too feeble-minded to understand what I am talking about does not mean I do not make sense," said Vargas. "Or did you think it was a coincidence that a huge beast just decided to ransack your city right before I confronted you?"

"So you brought that thing here?" Henry said through gritted, chattering teeth. "I guess it makes sense, but it certainly doesn't help your case. You could have killed everyone in the city, you son of a-"

"But I did not," said Vargas. "You must understand that I had to get some gauge of your potential. It was an unfortunate measure, but really for the greater good. If you could not handle a crisis situation like that, you would certainly not be able to handle a large-scale war. Fortunately, you proved your capability."

"How did you even know I would fight it? How did you know I wouldn't just run away or something?"

"An assumption. This is not the first time I have seen someone with your type of power. Based on my experiences, I assumed that between your innate sense of responsibility and, let us be honest, your desire to actually put your power to some sort of use, you would react. And you reacted quite well, I must say."

"Well, I'm flattered. But I'm still not helping you."

"You know, you really should be grateful. I gave you the opportunity to be a hero, to prove yourself to these people. And you did it. I would wager that if you disappeared right now, you would be a legend."

"Maybe. Or I might just be known as the fraud who blew up downtown and disappeared."

"Yes, I suppose that is a possibility."

"Anyway," said Henry, "the only one that's doing any disappearing around here is you. Now please-"

"When are you going to understand that this is not negotiable?" said Vargas. "You are coming with me, even if I have to haul your badly beaten-"

Henry threw a punch with his right fist, aiming right between Vargas's eyes. Vargas dodged it, and Henry was thrown off balance, barely keeping his footing. Shifting his weight to his toes, he pushed himself backwards, simultaneously uppercutting clumsily with his left fist. Vargas also dodged this, and punched Henry. Henry tried to dodge the blow, which only grazed him on the shoulder. After a slight stumble backwards, Henry desperately launched himself into the air.

"Hmm," said Vargas, watching Henry's ascent.

From his vantage point in the sky, Henry huffed and puffed and racked his brain. Obviously, this guy was determined to get Henry to go with him. Was he really from another dimension? Henry supposed it didn't really matter at this point; wherever he was from, Vargas was disturbingly strong and apparently quite determined. If I'm going to beat him, Henry thought, I'm going to have to catch him by surprise.

The moment Henry's feet hit the earth, he dashed headlong at Vargas. He poured all the energy he could muster into a furious assault. Vargas attempted to sidestep him, but Henry managed to land several blows to Vargas's torso and midsection. Furious punches fell like leathery hail, but Vargas was unfazed; it was as though Henry was trying to damage a marble statue by snapping a wet towel at it. Despair began to gnaw away in Henry's gut. The most galling thing was Vargas's demeanor during the attack. His face betrayed no anger or even annoyance; rather, he affected an air of bored indifference, as if Henry was reciting some particularly dull poetry rather than trying to beat him to a pulp. This indifference just made Henry angrier, and the angrier he grew, the more intense and sloppy his punches became.

Vargas's hand shot out and gripped Henry's throat. A sickening gurgling emanated from Henry's clenched jaw as Vargas lifted his from his feet and threw him into a tall pine tree. The tree trunk splintered on impact, and the top half of the tree fell on top of Henry, covering him with its boughs.

"Your foolish resistance is both annoying and heartening," said Vargas. "But I suppose you are going to force my hand." As Henry shoved his way out of the thick tangle of pine branches, Vargas planted his feet firmly and glared at him. He mumbled something and swung his arm in Henry's direction, fingers spread wide. To Henry's immense surprise, the tree enveloping him exploded into flames. The force of the explosion knocked Henry free of the blazing mess, but the spontaneous combustion made his blood run cold.

His face expressionless, Vargas mumbled some more and gestured again. Another explosion followed, right in front on Henry, the sheer force of it bowling him over. As he rolled away in a panic, the earth beneath him exploded again, laying him violently on his back. Despite himself, Henry screamed, a formless wail of shock and despair.

Vargas walked over to Henry, spare bits of stone and branch crackling under his feet. He loomed over the boy's prone body and said, "Are you finished with your tantrum?"

Henry wrapped his legs around Vargas's like pincers and began relentlessly pounding on him. Vargas grunted and smashed Henry's face into the ground. He then grabbed Henry by the throat once more and lifted him up. He punched Henry twice in the ribs, causing him to bounce in midair like a fleshy punching bag. He then lifted Henry even higher, then released his grip on Henry's throat. Henry fell for a millisecond, then felt the crushing impact of Vargas's fist against his cheek as he was hit in midair. He hit the ground several feet away with a dull thud, his hands slapping together upon impact. Dust particles settled on his rapidly coagulating blood.

"Wait…wait," Henry weakly choked out, holding up his left hand. "Hold on."

"I have done enough waiting, do you not think?" said Vargas, his eyes skyward.

"I mean…OK," said Henry. "I can't beat you. I give up."

"So you will go with me, then?"

"I just…listen, if I'm going to have to go with you, for God knows how long, will you at least let me say goodbye to my family?"

"Family?" Vargas said slowly, his eyebrow raised. "Well…"

"Just give me a few days," said Henry after spitting out a mouthful of crimson goop. It caught in midair a few centimeters from his mouth. He grunted and touched his hands together, hoping Vargas wouldn't recognize the reaction created by contact between his gloves. The blood instantly dropped to the ground and spattered. "What's today? Thursday? How about until next Friday? Let me tie up the loose ends, let people know where I'm going."

"I do not really have time-" said Vargas, seemingly oblivious to whatever Henry was doing.

"Look, I'll be a much better soldier if you'd just at least give me some time to say my goodbyes. Besides, I'm clearly not going without a fight if you try to take me today, and the beating you'd have to lay down on me in order to go with you would probably take me far more than eight days to heal from."

"I suppose it would be better for your morale," Vargas sighed, scratching his chin.

"Yeah, yeah," said Henry. "Exactly. Give me eight days. Meanwhile, you can relax, take a look around. I'm sure you wouldn't mind a bit of a vacation from constant warfare."

"A week and a day," said Vargas. He peered at the earth, motionless. Several moments passed, each a separate eternity. "Fine. I will allow you this. Eight days, and not a moment more. But rest assured that when your time is up, I will come for you. There will be no further delays."

"Got it."

"And I would not bother trying to run and hide if I were

you," said Vargas. "Your aura reeks of magic. I can find you anywhere, at any time. Remember that."

"Of course."

"Eight days," said Vargas. He turned and walked away. Henry lay on his back, aching as he stared up at the immense clouds drifting in front of the sun. Pain roared through his body in a panic, trying to be everywhere at once. Henry could hear Vargas's heavy footsteps trudging away; then all was silence, save for a bird chirping, and the occasional crackle of smoldering embers.

"Henry, my God," said Henry's dad, rising from the couch as the battered form of his son ambled into the house. "You look like hell. What happened to you?"

"I'd really rather not get into it," said Henry. "Suffice it to say I got beat up."

"What? But how is that even possible?" said Henry's father. "You just took on a huge snake monster and were barely scratched."

"I remember," said Henry.

"Then how-"

"Later," said Henry. "Please. I just need to clean myself up right now."

Henry stalked upstairs and headed for his bathroom. He growled at his reflection; his face was swollen and caked with dried blood. Dirt blanketed his face and clothes, and ash was smeared across his forehead. Pine needles and sundry filth had taken up residence in the rat's nest formerly known as his hair. He could not shower quickly enough.

Taking stock of himself as the shower's hot water caused steam to curl up around him, Henry noticed his fair share of obvious injuries. He had a large bruise on his torso that was likely only going to get worse, and a number of smaller scrapes and bruises. Overall, though, he was able to breathe and move relatively painlessly, so apparently nothing was broken. And despite the blood leaking from his mouth earlier, he had not coughed up any since, so the likelihood of internal bleeding was minimal. He had walked away in relatively good shape considering the beating he had taken, but that was no great consolation to him. The real damage was psychological; his pride was shattered, and he no longer felt the confidence of being the world's strongest man. Worst of all was the fact that he had approximately one week to figure out some way to avoid being forcibly snatched away into another dimension. It was a concern he never would have thought he would have, and he longed for the days of such ignorance. For a formerly illusory problem, it was certainly significant now.

When he got out of the shower, Henry grabbed an ice pack from the freezer and laid it over his face as he got into bed. He figured he probably wouldn't sleep well, but at least he might be able to reduce his facial swelling. He was not looking forward to the reaction at school tomorrow. He had just gotten people to believe his claims of unbelievable might; now that he had so clearly gotten thrashed by someone or something, his claims of superpowers would be all the more dubious.

Lying on his back with his eyes closed, Henry saw vague phantoms floating behind his eyelids. The bitter cold of the icepack stung his tender flesh as memories of his beating provoked a full-body chill. He heard a knock on his door, and grunted permission to enter.

“Henry?” said a small voice, nearly absorbed by the whining creak of the door opening. “Can I speak with you?”

“Of course, grandma,” said Henry, hardly moving. “If you don’t mind talking to a human glacier.”

“Henry, there’s something…well, I wanted to talk to you about something that concerns me.”

“Sure. What is it?”

“Your mother was telling me about your…about the changes you’ve been going through. About the powers.”

“Yeah, pretty cool, isn’t it?” said Henry. He shifted his weight onto a bruise and wheezed as a sharp pain rippled through his chest.

“This isn’t the first time something like this has happened, you know,” said Henry’s grandmother, sitting down on the edge of his bed. “I mean, I never really believed the stories. I thought they were things my mother was making up, nonsense to get me to quiet down. But now, I’m not so sure.”

“What do you mean?”

"My mother used to tell me about an ancestor of ours, years ago, who became very strong for a time. Stronger than you could ever imagine. Well, maybe *you* could imagine, but, you know, stronger than a normal person could imagine. Nothing good ever came of it. In fact, terrible things happened to that man and his family, and now that I see what's happening with you…well, I can't help but worry about the end result of all this."

"I understand," said Henry. "And I appreciate your concern, I really do. But I'll be fine."

"That so?" said Henry's grandmother. "Because you don't look fine to me. You look like you got trampled by a rhinoceros."

Henry moved the icepack and looked his grandmother in the face. Her expression was grave and unsettling, and Henry put the ice pack back on his face. "It's OK. Nothing to worry about. Just a temporary setback. An accident, really."

Henry's grandmother sighed. Her craggy features darkened, and she pursed her lips. "Henry," she said, "have I ever told you the story of Lenny McGee?"

"Doesn't sound familiar," said Henry, shaking his head.

"What is it?"

"It's a story my parents used to tell me," he said. "It goes like this: once there was a small village in the middle of a valley. It was a peaceful village, and the inhabitants went about their lives relatively comfortably.

"Well, one day, things began to change. A strange wind began to howl through the village. It started off as no more than a breeze, but as the days went by it became stronger and stronger, fiercer and fiercer. No one knew where it came from: some said it was a punishment from God for some unknown sin. Others said it was the wails of angry ghosts, coming to take back a land built upon their corpses. Still others said it was nothing of the sort; it was just Mother Nature at work, a change in the weather; unpleasant, sure, but nothing supernatural. Regardless of the reason, the wind continued to howl, and its ferocity continued to grow.

"One by one, the villagers began to move away. The wind scared them, and it was starting to seriously damage their homes. If it got much worse, they thought, their houses might just blow away. Rather than face that, the villagers decided it was best to simply find a new home.

"One of the villagers, however, had a different idea. His name was Lenny McGee, and the wind did not frighten him. He said that the village was his rightful home, and he liked it there, and that nothing and no one could make him leave.

"'Ain't no wind going to blow my house down,' he would say. 'Just you wait and see. I'll be nice and safe.'

"As the other villagers trickled out, Lenny began to construct a wall around his house, to shield it from the wind. It was strong and sturdy, and did a very good job of blocking the wind. But it was not enough, not for long. The wind just grew stronger and stronger, and so, in response, Lenny McGee built his wall bigger and bigger, higher and higher. It was really quite a sight to see.

"Weeks went by. The wind got so strong that almost everyone had left. Tom McGavin, the second to last man in town, came by to see Lenny McGee.

"'I'm moving on,' said Tom. 'This wind has gotten to be too much for me. It doesn't want me here, and so I'm not fixin' to be here anymore. You'd better move away too, Lenny McGee, before the wind gets so strong it blows even your house down.'

"'Ain't no wind going to blow my house down,' said Lenny McGee. 'Just you wait and see. I'll be nice and safe.'

"Tom McGavin pleaded with Lenny to reconsider, but Lenny was having none of it. And so away went Tom McGavin, shaking his head as he carted his belongings off in search of a new home. Lenny McGee just shrugged, and went back to work on his wall.

"The wind just kept getting stronger, and the wall just kept getting bigger. It was hard work, but Lenny's home was safe. The wind whipped and whirled all around him, screeching and yowling, but he paid it no mind. He just built and built and built. After a while, you could hardly see the sun, the wall was so high.

"The wind was rabid at this point. Lenny McGee could not feel it, but oh, could he hear it. He stood by the wall and listened to the howling and watched all sort of things fly by his home, carried on to who-knows-where by that terrible wind. Lenny just laughed.

"'Ain't no wind going to blow my house down,' he said.

'Not now, and not ever.'

"All of a sudden, there was a terrible noise. The wind had reached an unheard of strength, and gusts beat like enormous leaden fists upon the wall. As Lenny stared up at his mighty creation, the wall began to shudder. Then, just like that, the wall tilted forward. The wind had become so powerful that the wall itself could no longer stand, and it tipped right on over with a horrendous crash.

"Lenny McGee had been right. The wind never blew his house down. But it was gone all the same."

Henry sat up in bed, pulling away the icepack. Beads of condensation loitered on his face. "That's pretty morbid for a children's story," said Henry. "I'm not even entirely sure what kind of lesson I'm supposed to take from that."

"Don't let your pride get the best of you," his grandmother said. "Know when to give up. I don't know what happened to you today, but whatever it was, please be careful. Don't endanger yourself. I don't know what I would do if you…if you died."

Henry hugged his grandmother for the first time in several

years. He had no particular aversion to hugging her specifically; he just wasn't much of a hugger. But he embraced her now, careful not to let her body brush up against his angrier wounds. "I know you worry because you care. And I truly appreciate that. But there's nothing to worry about," he said softly. "Things are going to turn out great, just you watch."

"I hope you're right," his grandmother said, rising with a bit of difficulty. "Good night, Henry," she said, and closed the door behind her.

Henry lay on his back, aching and anxious. "Lenny McGee," he scoffed, then grabbed his iPod and put on some music to drown out his thoughts.

"Wow, man," said Doug, sizing Henry up. "What the hell happened to you?"

"You wouldn't believe me if I told you," Henry muttered.

"Look, up until I saw you this morning, I was under the impression you were pretty much invincible. Now here you are looking like you got run over by the ugly truck. So please, try me."

"The ugly truck?" said Trent. "I didn't know that was an expression now."

The boys were sitting around their usual spot at lunch, but the arrival of Henry and his battered countenance shifted the mood to awkward pretty quickly. Though his efforts to reduce his facial swelling had paid off to some degree, the damage was nonetheless obvious; his left eye was squinty and ringed in purple, his bottom lip was split, and a vague bruise had formed on his cheek.

"OK, here goes," said Henry, sitting down. "Just try to wrap your head around this. So apparently, that monster that I fought the other day? Some guy named Vargas unleashed it onto the city purely as a test of my abilities."

"OK," said Trent.

"But how did he know about you? And how did he know you would beat it? How did he know you would even fight it in the first place?" said Albert.

"All valid questions," said Henry. "He assumed, he said."

"OK," said Trent.

"So this Vargas guy, he then tells me that since I passed his stupid test, he's going to enlist me in his personal army to fight some war alongside him. Oh, and he's from another dimension. Did I mention that? And he's going to pull me into this other dimension so I can help his side win the war."

"OK," said Trent.

"But you don't-" said Albert.

"Hold on," said Henry. "So of course, I was like, this guy is off his rocker, and I tried to ditch him and go home." He motioned to the various wounds across his face. "And that's when this happened."

"OK," said Trent.

"How could he do that, though?" said Albert. "Why didn't you just kick his ass or something?"

"I tried. Believe me, I tried," said Henry. He stared off into the distance. "There was nothing I could do. I hit him, and it barely fazed him. He hit me, and it felt like a freight train ran into me. You should see how bad my chest looks."

"No thanks," said Doug.

"But you don't really believe this guy's from another dimension, do you?" said Trent. "That's just insane."

"Insane it may be, but I don't really have any other choice but to believe it," said Henry. "It's the only thing that makes any sense. Well, alright, maybe it doesn't exactly make sense, but it is the only way I can possibly explain what's happened here. You should have seen this guy…he could like throw fireballs and everything!"

"Wow, like *Street Fighter*?" said Albert.

"This is ridiculous," said Trent.

"Look, Trent," said Henry. "I'm a lot of things, but I'm not really the lying type. And you can see the cuts and bruises for yourself…this would be going a bit far for a practical joke, don't you think?"

The group was silent. Bits and pieces of conversations other students were having, random shrieks of laughter, and the ambient hum of traffic noise all floated by as the group of boys tried to poke the thread of the conversation through the eye of the needle of awkwardness.

"Well then, I'm pissed that I missed a super brawl," said Trent. "I bet it was awesome."

"Yeah, actually," said Henry with a chuckle, "it kind of was. Would've been awesomer if I had won, though."

"So what now?" said Doug. "He kicked your ass, but you're still here."

"I've got a week," Henry said, sighing. "The best I could do was get him to agree to that. I've got a week until he comes back for me and takes me to God-knows-where to do God-knows-what. Or kills me. Whatever he's planning to do. One week."

"One week," said Doug. "That's not much time."

"Guess you're not going to the Halloween dance," said Albert.

"No, I guess not," said Henry.

"So that's it then?" said Doug. "A week from now you're going to be gone. And then nothing, you're just outta here."

"It's not exactly up to me," said Henry. "I don't want it to happen…but I don't know what to do."

"Fight back," said Doug. "I'm sure you can take him next

time."

"You don't understand," said Henry. "Whatever I did had no effect on him whatsoever. It was just…I couldn't…"

"You know what? Shut up," said Doug. "I can't believe you. One day you're the king of the world, lifting up cars, getting your name put on your sweatshirt, and now you've already given up completely."

"That's bull," said Henry. "I haven't given up. I'm just kind of at a loss. I mean, what would you do?"

"Me? I don't know," said Doug. "But I sure as hell wouldn't give up."

Before Henry could reply, an undersized freshman boy shuffled up to the group, eyes on the ground. "Are you…," he said, "are you the kid who can…who can lift cars and stuff?"

"Me?" said Henry, trying to look him in the eyes. "Yup. That's me."

"Can you…I mean, would you, maybe…I don't know, show me?"

"Show you?" said Henry. "Well, I'm not lifting another car,

if that's what you mean. The last thing I need is yet another trip to the principal's office."

"Oh, no. That's fine," said the boy, rummaging through his pockets. He pulled out a smooth, pale yellow stone and handed it to Henry. "Do you think you could, I don't know, break this or something? Just…I've never seen anything like it and I think it would be cool."

"No problem," said Henry. He held the stone up in the palm of his hand, then balled his fingers up into a tight fist. Muffled crunching sounds followed, and when Henry opened up his fist, nothing but white, chalky powder remained. As a soft breeze carried away bits of the yellow dust, the freshman went from gape-mouthed awe to a grin of pure satisfaction.

"That. Was. Awesome," he said.

"Yeah, can't argue with you there," Henry said with a smile and a shrug. "Anytime you need something crushed, just let me know."

"Thanks. Wow,' said the boy. "Oh, hey, one other thing."

"Yeah?"

"What happened to your face?"

"Beat it," said Doug. "We're busy."

The freshman boy scurried away as Doug turned toward Henry. "Did you see that?" Doug said. "That was amazing."

"What?" said Henry. "You already knew I could do stuff like that. You shouldn't be surprised."

"Not you, dummy," said Doug. "That kid. Have you ever in your life experienced anything like that? He was in *awe* of you, man! And look out there!" He pointed into the courtyard. "Do you see that?"

"What?" said Henry, squinting.

"Lunch boxes!" said Doug. "You've got a bunch of these idiots out there carrying lunchboxes because of *you*!"

"Aw, what're you talking about?" said Henry, fondling his lunchbox handle idly. "I'm sure those kids had lunchboxes before me."

"No. No," said Doug. "Nobody had lunchboxes before you. Nobody. You were the only one with a lunchbox, and you got ragged on for it. Remember?"

"Yes," Henry muttered.

"And now look," said Doug. "Lunchboxes. Only a few, but still. There they are. Look, that kid even has a L.E.B.S. lunchbox! And have you noticed how they look at you now? Have you noticed how they talk to you?"

"Well, of course, but-"

"No 'but,'" said Doug. "Do you even understand what's happening here? For the first time in forever, people are excited around here. They're excited about *you*!"

"Huh. You may have a point," said Henry.

"I would argue that part of the excitement is out of fear that another giant reptile is going to come flatten the city. Just my two cents," said Trent.

"You probably have a point, too," said Henry.

"Look, what I'm saying is this:" said Doug. "We are witnessing the dawn of something that is absolutely nuts. What's happening with you is something no one has ever seen before. Or at least that no one around here has ever seen before, as far as I know. Anyway, not to sound like a jerk or anything, but we're all a part of something incredible here. I dare say it's actually inspirational. And I just…I don't know, I don't want it to just be over with, just like that."

"And I understand that," said Henry. "Believe me, I feel the same way. More so. But is the excitement worth all of this? Is it worth downtown being flattened? Is it worth me being abducted and forced into slavery or whatever?"

"It just…it doesn't have to be that way. I know it doesn't. I…I believe in you, I guess," said Doug. "Wow. That was pretty awful, huh?"

"I think I'm gonna be sick," said Trent.

"Yeah, well, believing in myself didn't keep me from getting my ass kicked," Henry said with a sigh. "So if I'm going to get out of this, it's going to take more than confidence." As Henry said this, the bell signaling the end of lunch rang. "I'll see you guys later."

"We'll help you out, you know," said Albert.

"I would hope so," said Henry as he walked away. "But thanks."

As Henry walked to class, he noticed how everyone gave

him much more space than they ever had. Rather than shoving his way through the jabbering masses as he had so many times before, his approach caused the students to part ahead of him, opening up a narrow path, a luxury he was unfamiliar with but found fairly enjoyable. As he walked this path, he took note of the fact that most of the eyes he passed followed him intently, followed by whispers or the occasional hoot. He also noted a preponderance of lunchboxes where, perhaps, there had not been any several days prior. As he surveyed the situation, someone brushed up against his arm, and he instinctively whirled to face them.

"Hey, Henry," said Denise Hargrove, smiling up at him, though she flinched a bit at his speedy about-face. "I'm glad I saw you. I didn't get to talk to you this morning."

"*Get* to talk to me?" said Henry. "I wasn't aware that talking to me was a privilege."

Denise giggled. "Oh, don't be ridiculous. Hey, listen: were you planning on going to the Halloween dance?"

Henry's heart skipped at least one beat. "Um, why?" he asked, his voice raising by a fraction of an octave.

"Well, I was thinking," Denise said, "that maybe, if you're not already going with someone, maybe you could go with me."

Breathe, Henry, he thought to himself. "I thought you were going with Roderick, though," he said. He knew he was blushing and hated himself for it.

"Yeah, I mean, I am. Or I was," she said, rolling her eyes, "But he's just been such a jerk lately. Like, I've gotten really sick of it, honestly. And you've always been so sweet that I think it might be fun if we go together."

Henry was flabbergasted. Was this what it was like to have status? He had spent so much time as a semi-anonymous misanthrope that this sudden outpouring of beautiful, provocatively dressed goodwill was foreign and amazing. Sure, this turn of events might be solely due to his new powers and the attention resulting from them…but maybe not. In any case, it was Denise Hargrove asking him to the dance. Questioning that would be like peering down a gift horse's throat.

"I, uh, sure," said Henry, mentally chastising himself for his appalling sentence structure. "Yeah. Let's…OK. As long as you don't mind being seen with somebody sporting all this." He vaguely circled his face with his finger, pointing to his bruises.

"Just put a cold steak on it or something," said Denise. "No big deal. I mean, you've got like a week to heal."

A week. Henry's mind shifted into a nauseating, lightning-fast slide show of blood and fire, of agony and dirt, of Vargas's icy gaze. He winced and looked away from Denise with a muffled gasp.

"What?" she said, glancing over her shoulder.

"Oh, it's just that…um, I just remembered that I might not be able to go next week," Henry said sheepishly. "I do want to go with you, really I do. I'm just not sure if I'll be able to, and I'd rather tell you that now than have to cancel on you at the last minute."

"But why?" said Denise, a flash of anger darting across her bewildered eyes. "What's going on?"

"That's kind of a tough one," said Henry. "I don't want to lie to you, but if I tell you the truth, you'll probably think that I've lost my mind. Or be completely terrified. Either way, I think I'm better off just keeping that to myself for now. I wish I could just say yes, but it's not that simple."

Denise just stared at Henry for a moment. "I don't get you," she said finally.

"I'm sorry," said Henry. He wracked his brain for something else to say, something that could salvage the situation. He drew a blank, instead having a brief flashback to an awful afternoon early in his childhood where he almost drowned in a lake when the tide unexpectedly yanked him in. He recalled flailing impotently as his lungs filled with fluid until they felt like a pair of watermelons. Unable to raise his gaze from the ground, Henry muttered a hurried farewell and rushed off to class. The rush of confidence he had been feeling abated as quickly as it had manifested. He was thankful for the fact that the other students were giving him more room than before, if for no other reason than his compulsion to punch was reaching record highs.

"What happened to your face?" called a random voice.

Henry's mind clouded over with wicked fantasies.

The afternoon found Henry calmer, if no less achy.

Detention had passed by like a mundane dream, with Henry staring at the wall and letting his mind wander to all sorts of dark and peculiar places. He was oblivious to the stares and whispers of his fellow detainees, lost as he was in his morbid reverie. This daze was broken only by Mr Sadek's announcement that detention was over, and the students were free to go about their business, funny or otherwise.

As Henry slowly rose from his desk and shook off the remnants of his trance, Mr. Sadek had walked up to him and asked, "Are you…OK with this? I mean, are you happy?"

"Why would I be happy about detention?"

"Oh, I don't know," said Mr. Sadek. He was noticeably sweating. "I suppose that's not the right word. But you're not angry about it? You understand the fairness of it?"

"I guess. I don't know," said Henry. "I'd rather not do it, of course, but I'm getting used to it."

Mr. Sadek's eyes darted about like inebriated fireflies. "Well, you know, maybe you've gotten the point. Maybe…well, how about this? You've learned your lesson. You're fine. There's no need for you to come to detention anymore."

"Um, thanks," said Henry. He stared at the principal's sopping forehead. "What's going on with you, anyway, Mr. Sadek? You look like you've seen a ghost or a mutant or something."

"Nothing! Nothing," said Mr. Sadek. "Just want to make sure you're not…you know, angry. That you're OK."

"I'm just peachy, thanks," said Henry, "even though I don't quite get where all this is coming from."

"Good. Good. I just need to look out for the welfare of my school and my students. You understand."

"I'm not sure that I do. What are you trying to say, exactly?"

"Well, I know that you're not…unfamiliar with violence, exactly, and I just thought…"

"Never mind. Thanks for commuting my sentence."

"So…wait. Did my asking if you were angry make you angry? Are you angry now?"

"*No*. Have a good night."

"Um…Hope your face heals up," Mr. Sadek called as Henry exited the classroom.

Now Henry found himself in a familiar position, strolling through the woods, looking up at an uneasy evening sky that seemed unable to decide whether or not it felt like raining. The presence of the familiar was soothing, as the mounting oddness of Henry's life was taking a similarly mounting toll on him. Strange as superpowers and suspicious, well-dressed men and extra-dimensional assailants were, the woods were still the same.

Henry heard a lilting, bubbly whisper that let him know he was near the La Estigia river. The river was in actuality more of a stream, a serene, ever-flowing serpent that snaked throughout the woods in its eternal journey to the sea. The recent rains had the river at its highest point since the spring, but it still flowed calmly, with a gentle murmur.

One fall day when he was nine years old, Henry had been romping through these woods, enjoying the lack of supervision he had only recently been allowed some degree of. He was headed to the river, which he had long harbored a not-entirely-explicable affection for. As sunlight filtered through the boughs above him and the cicadas sang their shrill melody, Henry had happened upon the corpse of a robin. It almost looked fake, lying on the ground motionless, its swollen breast blood red, its eyes wide open yet staring at nothing. Grimly fascinated, Henry knelt down and brushed his forefinger against the corpse. It was, naturally, unresponsive.

Henry had never actually seen death before. Sure, he had seen people get shot on television and murdered scores of aliens in various video games, but an actual, tangible corpse had thus far eluded him. As Henry's gaze passed over the robin's smooth, dirty feathers, his fascination grew. Gently, he slipped his hand beneath the corpse.

The unseen portion of the bird contained a texture Henry was not prepared for. A slick, slimy wetness met his fingertips, mixed with scattered grit and hard bits of something. His eyes widened, but Henry persisted in placing the bird with his hand and lifting it. Squishy moisture pooled on his palm as Henry held the robin with as much care as he could muster. Its wide black eyes seemed to hold some secret Henry was not privy to, and he was unsure whether he wanted to know it in any case.

Henry carried the bird with him, holding it as delicately as a porcelain doll filled with explosives, as he approached the river. The La Estigia's familiar murmur met his ears as he laid his eyes upon the bank. After standing there for few moments, observing the water rush by playfully as the early autumn breeze swept its ephemeral fingers through his short hair, Henry stared back down at the robin's corpse. He gasped; his fascination had suddenly turned into revulsion, and his stomach churned as his mouth twisted into a pouty scowl. Filled with abrupt panic, he hurled the corpse in the river, and watched it bob on the surface of the water for a little while, until it vanished further downstream. When the bird's corpse was gone, Henry looked back down at his hands. They were coated with sticky brown blood, with a few dark bits of offal and yellowish-white bone fragments intermingled with the viscous fluid. He thrust his hands into the waters of the La Estigia, rubbing them together beneath the flowing water. Dark tendrils snaked away from his hands, rushing away to join the robin in its watery grave.

Now, seven years later, Henry stood upon the banks of the

La Estigia once more. He stared down at this hands, clad in Jeremiah Garrison's enchanted leather gloves. With a sigh, he slowly peeled the gloves off and held them, balled-up, in his right fist.

Maybe this was all a huge mistake, he thought. This had been fun for a while, but maybe I'm not supposed to have this power. Maybe no one is. And maybe the most responsible thing to do is to throw these damn gloves in the river and go back to the way things used to be.

Henry's mind raced. He thought of the rush he had felt when he first discovered these powers, of Doug's amazement when Henry first showed him his abilities. Of his victory over Vargas's pet monster, of the sudden proliferation of lunchboxes at school. Of Denise Hargrove. But he also thought of Vargas, his cold eyes and galling arrogance, and whatever hell he was capable of carrying over with him from wherever he was really from. Henry's ribs ached at the very thought of his mysterious assailant. His teeth gritted in anger. It would be hilarious, he thought, if Vargas had gone to all this trouble just to return and find me just some weak, normal dude.

Weak, normal dude. The way things used to be. Is that really a place he wanted to be? Henry recalled his urine-soaked uniform, his broken Nintendo, his contempt for the guys who had cars and girlfriends. He recalled a time, which seemed so distant, when Roderick had occupied the role of an insurmountable obstacle instead of a bitter joke. Did he really want to go back there? Looking downstream, he realized that even if he tossed the gloves into the water and watched them wash away, he would have no guarantee that someday, whether it be tomorrow or a century in the future, someone else wouldn't find the gloves. And if and when someone did, what guarantee did Henry have that whoever found them wouldn't abuse them, or sell them to someone who would put the might they granted to nefarious use? Like it or not, this power was his responsibility to keep watch over, if nothing else. And how better to keep the power safe and secure than by wielding it?

And besides all of that, Henry thought, having superpowers is really, really awesome.

Henry wriggled his hands back into the leather gloves and breathed deeply. He pulled his cell phone out of his pocket and dialed Doug's number,

"Hi Doug," he said.

"Hey, man. What's up?"

"If you don't mind," Henry said, the rising wind whipping around him, the La Estigia gurgling seductively in the background, "I'd like it if you could call up Albert and Trent, and see if the four of us can meet up. I think it's about time we put our heads together and figured out how I'm going to beat this Vargas bastard."

"That's m'boy," said Doug.

Chapter Eight

"Here's what we know," said Henry. He was pacing around his room as Doug, Albert and Trent stared at him. "Vargas is super strong. Super fast. More so than I am. He pretty much shrugs off anything I throw at him. He keeps, or kept, a huge snake dragon monster thing for a pet. And he can apparently generate fire or something with his hands, which maybe worries me the most because it makes me wonder what else he might be able to do that I haven't seen and probably would never expect. In short, he's a house, and I have no real idea the extent of what he's capable of. Have I missed anything?"

"Does that Nintendo work?" said Trent, pointing at the Nintendo Entertainment System Henry had purchased at the flea market and long since given up on.

"What?" said Henry. "Oh. Well, I'm not sure I understand the relevance of the question, but no, I don't think it does. At least,

I haven't been able to get it to work."

"Let me try," said Trent, crouching down in front of the video game system. "I bet I can get it going."

"Your dedication is really mind-boggling," said Henry, eyes rolling.

"Tell me about it," said Trent, slamming his fist down on the top of the machine.

"You know, in a way, I guess that is sort of relevant, because I was thinking about it today," said Albert, "and I think this Vargas guy is like, you know, a boss for you to fight."

"A boss? Whose boss?" said Doug.

"What I mean is, think of it like a video game," said Albert. "In a video game, OK, you've got your boss characters. Now the boss is tough; a conventional offense normally won't work against him…it'll just get you killed. But the boss usually has a weak point, and if you can figure out what that is, and gear your attack to exploit it, then you can beat him."

"Right," said Trent. "Then the question is, what is his weak point?"

"Or points. He might have more than one," said Doug.

"Either way," said Trent, inserting a game cartridge into the Nintendo, "we've got to figure it out."

"Or figure *them* out," said Doug.

"I don't suppose there are any parts of his body that flash bright red or anything," said Trent. He clicked the power button on the Nintendo several times, with no results. "Is this thing even plugged in?"

"I think so. Jeez, who cares right now?" said Henry. "Can we focus here?"

"I am focused. I'm on a level of focus so high that you can't even comprehend it," said Trent.

"Let's think about this. What exactly did you do to Vargas? What methods of attack did you use, so we know what worked and what didn't?" said Albert. His cell phone beeped, and he flipped it open. "Excuse me," he said, and began typing out a text message to someone.

"Let's see," said Henry, scratching the back of his neck. "There was a whole lot of *didn't*. Mainly I tried to punch him a lot.

Plenty of them didn't connect, but the ones that did didn't even rattle him. He said he was wearing armor, and even though I have to say it didn't look like any sort of armor I've ever seen, it provides some heavy-duty protection. It must be pretty damn tough to penetrate."

Doug chuckled.

"What?" said Henry.

"Nothing. Nothing," said Doug. "Penetrate," he whispered with a giggle.

"You guys…" said Henry, rubbing the bridge of his nose.

"Where did you punch him?" said Albert. "The times you successfully hit him, where did the punches land?"

"Chest, mostly. I guess," said Henry.

"Chest. Which was obviously armored. Did you hit him in the face, or anywhere on the head, really?"

"I'm not sure. I don't think so, though. I tried, but he dodged all of those punches, as far as I can remember."

"Alright. Interesting. And the armor he was wearing…was he wearing any sort of helmet or anything?" said Albert. His phone beeped again, and he went back to typing another text message.

"Nope. A head with hair and all the usual features. That's all he had above the neck."

"So that could be a weak point," said Doug. "Because no matter who this guy is or what he's made of, I'd have to think a good sock in the jaw from a guy that can lift a car is gonna mess him up fairly proper."

"Which is most likely why he only would have avoided your attacks aimed at his head and just absorbed everything else," said Albert. "So, by the boss principal, we have a potential weakness."

"OK, keep that in mind, then: focus on the head," said Doug, tapping his index finger against his skull.

"So many jokes I could make…" said Trent. He blew into the bottom of the Nintendo cartridge.

"Of course, my efforts to focus on the head didn't work out so well the first time," said Henry with a sigh. He slumped against the wall. "I don't know how I'm going to slow him down enough to where I can actually land a solid hit to the cranium. I guess I could try to dump a barrel of molasses on him or something."

"Tar. Concrete. Particularly thick oatmeal," said Doug. "Maybe you can bog him down in melodrama."

"That's just weird," said Henry.

"How about if, instead of slowing him down, you speed yourself up? What about that?" said Albert, typing away on his phone.

"How exactly am I supposed to do that?" said Henry, eyebrows arched. "Do you have some spare syringes full of adrenaline that I'm not aware of?"

"Well, no. But I figured we may as well explore our options."

"Maybe. But that option's a dead end, far as I'm concerned," said Henry. "I've already got superpowers…I don't know how reasonable it is to ask for me to get even *more* powerful. It's like asking a supermodel to get more beautiful."

"Jeez. Arrogant, much?" said Doug.

"I don't mean it like that," Henry snapped. "I'm just trying to be logical, is all. If you have some conceivable way for me to noticeably increase my speed within the space of the next few days,

I'm all ears. Otherwise, let's move on."

"What the hell did you do to this thing?" said Trent, shaking the Nintendo. "This is ridiculous."

"Apparently, some of us have already moved on," said Henry.

"So one thing I want to know about is this fire you said he shot at you, or whatever he did," said Albert, his eyes briefly rising from his cell phone. "What exactly was that? How did he do it?"

"As far as the how…don't know," said Henry. "As in, I don't know what the hell was going on there, if he had some sort of tiny flame thrower or if he was doing something else entirely. Basically, what I remember was a look of intense concentration on his face, a gesture, and then fire. Oh, and he said something or another, real low so I couldn't hear it, but I don't know if that had anything to do it. For all I know, he was reciting a recipe for fudge brownies to himself. Or calling me a really bad name."

"I could tell you which is more likely," said Doug. He looked over at Trent, who was hunched over the Nintendo, slapping it and hissing curses. "Wow, man. It's just like watching ancient man trying to harness the power of fire."

"That's strange. The Vargas thing," said Albert. "Yeah, maybe he does have like a tiny flamethrower or something. I mean, if he has that armor, and if he can cross between dimensions, anything's possible. He could easily have access to advanced weaponry like that."

"Maybe," said Henry, staring out his window at the starless evening sky, overlaid by the ghostly reflections of the four friends. "But there was something Vargas said before he really started beating on me, when he was making his little sales pitch to me, about magical energies or some such thing. And between that, and the fact that what I witnessed with my own eyes doesn't make one damn bit of sense, I'm a little concerned that I'm dealing with something a bit more bizarre than advanced weaponry."

"Magical energies?" said Doug. "I'm sorry, I don't mean to trivialize this, but that sounds really stupid."

"Ordinarily, I'd be inclined to agree with you," said Henry. "Totally stupid. But I don't really know what to believe anymore, and if I can do the things I'm capable of, I have to believe that this guy might have abilities I can't even fathom. And if that's the case…well, I'd be lying if I told you I didn't find the idea of black magic being used against me to be fairly disturbing."

"I really want to see this guy," said Albert. "I mean, all these things you're telling us…I know it's dumb, but I really want to experience, or witness, I guess, what you're talking about. I just…when else am I going to get the chance to see something like this?"

"I wish I could share your enthusiasm," said Henry. "But I guess I probably would if I wasn't on the verge of being pummeled and kidnapped. However, since I am, I'm actually hoping nothing particularly cool happens."

"Or rather, that if something cool happens, it ends in you winning," said Doug with a grim smirk.

"Pretty much."

"OK, so we have one potential weakness as his head. And…um, no others. So far. And we have to leave open the possibility that he knows magic, in which case he is literally capable of anything and may be able to kill you with an incantation and a gesture," said Albert. "The more I look at it…"

"…the more screwed I seem to be," said Henry. He sighed, and cocked his head at Albert. "Who do you keep text messaging, anyway?"

"Hmm? Oh," he said. His face instantly flushed red. "It's, ah, Jenny. She just wants to, ah, know about my day and stuff. No big deal."

"Young love," said Doug, with an exaggerated tilt of his head and clasp of his hands.

"Good for you, man," said Henry, nodding at Albert. Then he groaned and put his head in his hands, "Oh God, I can't believe I rejected Denise Hargrove! What the hell is wrong with me?"

"Impending doom, I'd say," said Doug.

"Sounds about right," said Trent. He turned back to the Nintendo. "I think somebody cast some black magic on *this* thing."

"I think these past few weeks have just been a cruel joke," said Henry.

"I'll trade you," said Trent.

"Like hell."

"At least you've got something going for you," said Trent. "Even if your powers do end up ruining your life, they're still pretty awesome. What have any of us got?"

"Speak for yourself," said Doug.

"We'll see how awesome it ends up being," said Henry. "I just don't know how I'm going to do this."

"If you could just get rid of his armor, I think you'd have a pretty good chance, black magic or no," said Albert. "But as it is, it looks like you've just got to do whatever you can to attack his only obvious vulnerability."

"Or just drop a piano on him," said Doug.

"Best advice I've heard all day," said Henry. As he said this, he glanced under his bed. Amongst the shadows and crumpled articles of dirty laundry, he could vaguely make out the corner of the worn wooden box he had removed from the attic so recently, when life was safe and mundane and utterly galling. Henry suddenly recalled the metallic horror within the box, the unassuming cylinder that unfolded into pure death. Henry was tempted to open up the box as the idea of the scythe nagged at him vaguely, almost whispering to him to just take it out, take it out of the box and show it to his friends. Show them that maybe, just maybe he did have a weapon potent enough to combat futuristic armor and possible sorcery. Show them salvation in the form of the reaper. A new plan began to take shape within Henry's head, a series of actions in which this awful relic might just be of some use to him in overcoming Vargas's seeming invincibility.

But it wasn't that simple. Henry's resolution to keep the source of his powers a secret from his friends was unchanged. He could only imagine the pandemonium that would ensue if anyone were to figure out the destructive potential of his gloves. Someone, and more than likely several someones, would no doubt seek to relieve him of the gloves, which would then lead to him either having to fight to retain possession of them or to accept responsibility for the actions of whoever the new owner would be. To say nothing of the fact that he simply wouldn't be special anymore.

Were Henry to show the scythe to his friends, he would have to answer the inevitable barrage of questions: what it is, where it came from, etc. He had a fairly strong distaste for the idea of lying to his friends, and besides, conceiving a believable lie concerning the scythe's appearance would doubtless be a Herculean task. Yet if he told them the truth about the scythe's origins (or at least as much as he knew about it), he would have to tell them about the box and the journal and…it was an unreasonably slippery slope. It was better not to mention the scythe whatsoever, as far as his friends were concerned. But that did not mean that Henry could not utilize the scythe for himself when the fated hour arrived, and for the first time since suffering the humiliating beating at the hands of Vargas, Henry felt ever so slightly optimistic. Excited, even.

"Hello? Henry?" said Doug, waving his hand in front of Henry's face. "What's up? What are you looking at?" He leaned forward and looked down.

"Nothing," said Henry, his gaze darting away from the shadows beneath his bed. "My mind was wandering. I'm just tired, I guess."

"Well, hey! Good news," said Trent.

Henry turned to see the familiar image of the title screen of

Super Mario Bros. taking up residence of his television screen. The Nintendo's power light emanated a warm red glow. "How did you do that?" he said. "I thought it was a lost cause."

"No such thing," said Trent, picking up a controller. "You just gotta keep trying."

"Hope springs eternal," said Albert.

"Yeah, sure. What the hell," said Trent. "Now, who wants to be player two?"

The next morning was bright and clear, and peculiarly warm for that time of year. Downtown St. Dante was a mess of out-of-town cops and construction workers, taking advantage of the nice weather by beginning to repair some of the damage done to the city by the introduction of unbridled chaos. For his part, Henry was groggy and irritable, having been plagued by gruesome nightmares that had dissipated like hissing fog the instant he opened his eyes, save for the exhaustion that follows prolonged terror. His eyes were barely open, casting the world into a grainy haze before him, as he shrugged on his personalized sweatshirt over a plain white t-shirt.

"You don't need that sweatshirt this morning, dear," his mother said as he opened the front door to leave for school. "It's going to be really warm today."

Henry mumbled something about effective branding and lurched out into the blazing morning. He shaded his eyes with his right hand and, as he adjusted to the searing brightness, he noticed the forms of two men, impeccably clad in dark suits, standing on the sidewalk outside his home. He instantly recognized them as the two men he had seen at the construction site days ago, the same men who showed up right after he had defeated the enormous monster and who had been tracking him ever since. For a moment, Henry thought about making a run for it; however, since these men apparently knew who he was at this point, or at least where he lived, he quickly realized that an escape attempt would ultimately be merely delaying the inevitable. So instead, he shook his head to clear some of the cobwebs and approached the men.

"Henry Garrison?" said the younger man.

"That's me," Henry said with a slight wince. "Morning."

"Tom Tyker," said the younger man, extending his hand.

The sun reflected off his blonde hair, making his head a veritable corona that was difficult for Henry to look directly at; he thrust out his hand blindly and hoped for the best. Tyker had the bone-crushing grip of a man trying just a wee bit too hard to prove himself. Henry resisted the urge to respond with a bone-crushing grip of his own.

The older man stepped forward and extended his hand with a cough. "James Foley," he said gruffly as he squeezed Henry's hand firmly, yet gently. Henry responded in kind as Mr. Foley said, "It's a pleasure to finally meet you. Mind if we talk for a minute?"

"No, not really," said Henry. "But I've got to get to school, so can we walk and talk?"

"Well-" said Tyker.

"Absolutely," said Foley with a sweeping gesture towards the sidewalk. "After you."

A cardboard skeleton and various freshly carved jack-o-lanterns grinned at the trio from an otherwise empty porch as they walked by. Tyker snorted and said, "I'm glad we're finished with this little wild goose chase. Not really the best use of my time."

"We've spent quite a bit of energy trying to find you," said Foley, looking around him as he walked. "For a small town, it's been remarkably difficult to locate you, despite your…reputation, as it were."

"Hmm," said Henry. "Mind telling me who it was that tipped you off?"

"'Fraid not," said Tyker. "Our sources always stay confidential. Security purposes. You understand."

"Figured," said Henry. He nervously glanced at his lunchbox, which today emanated a slight metallic rattle on top of the usual thump of lunch items sliding around in there. He had dropped the metallic cylinder from the box beneath his bed into his lunchbox before heading out this morning, and it currently had a turkey sandwich draped over it. Henry hoped the men weren't going to search him.

"We're not here to kill you or anything, if that's what you think. Not yet, anyway," Tyker said with a odd, hoarse laugh as he slapped Foley on the back.

"Tom has a…unique sense of humor," said Foley. "But he's

right; there's no reason for you to be afraid of us."

"Who said I was?" said Henry.

"Oooh," said Tyker. "A feisty one."

"What I mean is, our visit here is actually a very positive thing for you," said Foley, scratching his mustache. "Potentially, anyway. Depending on how things go, we just might have a very lucrative opportunity for you."

"Like what?" said Henry.

"We'll get to that," said Tyker. "But first of all, just so I know we're not wasting even more of our time in this God-forsaken town than we already have, we're going to need you to answer a few questions for us."

"In that case, let me save you some time. That big old monster that you guys took away to God-knows-where? Yes, I took it down single-handedly. No, I have no idea what it was or where it came from, or rather I have some idea, but you look like reasonable guys and my thoughts on the matter are probably a little far-fetched for reasonable people to accept as anything other than, I don't know, pure insanity. Finally, as to the elephant in the room, I do have what I suppose you'd refer to as 'superpowers,' including enhanced speed, strength and toughness, and am unsure as to the source of these abilities or why they manifested in me and no one else. Basically."

"Well, that definitely helps," said Foley. "We more or less suspected all of that, but it's still good to hear you confirm it."

"So you actually believe me?"

"Of course we believe you. This is the sort of thing we deal with," said Tyker. "You don't think it was a coincidence that we arrived at the scene of the disturbance so soon after it unfolded, do you? Admittedly, we weren't expecting the creature to be beaten into submission when we showed up, but in our line of work there's not much room for disbelief."

"I think, really, the biggest question is this: when did these powers of yours manifest?" said Foley. He had pulled a small notepad out of his jacket pocket and was jotting something down in it.

"Um, I'm not one hundred percent sure," said Henry, "since I might have had them for a little while and not realized it.

But a couple weeks ago, I guess. I sort of figured it out by accident, broke some things I shouldn't have. But yeah, couple of weeks."

"And were there any unusual circumstances surrounding the emergence of these powers?" asked Tyker. Sweat was beading on his forehead and his tone of voice was becoming increasingly irritable. "Did anything happen out of the ordinary, around the same time you started noticing your abilities?" He pulled off his sunglasses. "Friggin' moisture," he grumbled, and rubbed his folded-over tie on the lenses before putting the glasses back on.

"Unusual circumstances?" said Henry. Sure, he thought. I found a pair of magic gloves and a futuristic killing implement in a box in my attic. "No, not really. I mean, I moved with my parents, into my grandmother's house. But none of them got superpowers out of it, so I don't know how much good that information does you."

"I see," said Tyker. "And don't you think it's an awfully big coincidence that right around the same time you mysteriously find yourself endowed with superhuman strength, a similarly unbelievable monster would just appear out of the blue and start wreaking havoc in your town? Just in your opinion."

"Mister," said Henry, staring at his reflection in Tyker's sunglasses, "It is an awfully big coincidence. Emphasis on the awful. It's been bugging me for days. All I know is, I was walking home from school and found myself in the middle of a nightmare. Now I can sit here and try to figure out the timing and logic behind the whole thing, but honestly, I'd prefer just to be thankful that I was there at that time and powerful enough to do something about it."

"But surely you'll admit that you can be both thankful *and* inquisitive? That they're not mutually exclusive?" said Tyker.

"Tom and I are just trying to figure this out," said Foley gently, stepping in front of his partner. "We're just trying to piece together a logical explanation for this chain of events, that's all. As you can probably imagine, there are some very important people who are quite interested in you and what you seem to be able to do. Our job is to get to the bottom of this whole deal."

"I understand that," said Henry. "All I'm saying is, let me know when you find out anything. Because at this point in time, I'm not the guy to ask for answers."

"Alright. Of course. This whole ordeal must have been very stressful for you," said Foley. "But if it makes you feel any better, we might have a…well, I guess you could call it a job opening for you. If you're interested. I mean, it's not every day that someone with your skill set emerges, and we can put you to very good use. You'd be helping out your country, and we'd make sure you were compensated for it, of course."

"Here we go," said Henry. He turned and faced Foley with gritted teeth. "If you're out to recruit me to be some sort of super-assassin for the government, I'm not going to do it. I'm not a murderer, and I'm not going to be used as someone's attack dog. I'm sorry, I know about patriotism and all that, but I'm not killing anybody."

"I'm glad to hear it," said Foley as Tyker snorted. "Henry, have you ever met an assassin? An honest-to-goodness assassin? They're scum. Cold degenerates with no more regard for a human life than one might have for shredded Kleenex. They're eccentric sociopaths that may have to be terminated themselves at any moment, if they don't hang themselves from the rafters first. Now, you've shown yourself to be an immensely powerful force in just a few days, and heaven knows what you may be capable of in the long run. Do you really think, for one solitary minute, that it would be in anybody's best interest to take a boy who can pick up construction vehicles and turn him into an unfeeling, bloodthirsty lunatic? It would be immensely shortsighted, to say the least."

Henry felt oddly disappointed. "Well then, what are you talking about? What can I do?"

"Well, take this situation the other day with that creature," said Foley. "We're happy you were there to handle that. It saved us quite a bit of effort."

"But we could have done it ourselves, if need be, and we were certainly prepared to" said Tyker. "Not a problem. Done it before."

"Before? Like when?" said Henry, stopping in his tracks.

"It's nothing you would have heard about," said Tyker. "That's what we're here for. The containment of unusual situations and the prevention of public panic. We wouldn't be doing our jobs if you knew about anything that we do. I mean, there's the odd crank magazine article, but no one takes those things seriously anyway."

"So do you guys like cover up aliens and stuff? Like UFOs and everything? Is that stuff actually real?"

"Well, of course UFOs are real," said Tyker, rolling his eyes. "The term means 'Unidentified Flying Object.' If I said UFOs weren't real, I would be saying that no one has ever been unable to identify something they say in the sky. Obviously, that's not true. Basic logic."

"But as far as space aliens and such," said Foley, "no, they're not real. At least as far as we know, and thankfully so. We have more than enough issues with earthbound phenomena as it is."

"Tell me about it," said Tyker.

"So what? Monsters and all that?" said Henry. The sheer bizarreness of the conversation was starting to awaken him. Apparently monster talk put caffeine to shame.

"Maybe. Who knows?" said Foley. "Basically, we'd just like

to have you on-call, in a manner of speaking. If a situation arose like the one you dealt with downtown, it would be marvelously helpful if we had your assistance. It would make our lives a lot easier."

"And how is this any different from making me an assassin?" said Henry. "I'd still be killing for money."

"Monsters are not people, Henry. Though people can sometimes be monsters," Foley said with a chuckle.

"What does that even mean?" asked Henry.

"Besides that," Foley continued, "who said anything about you killing things? Most of the time, we don't want our quarry dead; there's much more to be learned from live specimens. That's not really our department, though. We just bag 'em and dump them in someone else's lap."

"I don't know," said Henry. "I just feel kind of weird about the whole thing. I mean, I don't even really know who you guys are, for one, and besides that, it just seems kind of sketchy to me."

"It's a lot to absorb, I know," said Foley. "You don't have to make any decisions right now. To be honest, I don't officially have the authority to make you any binding offer at this point anyway. Tom and I are heading out of town tonight, but we should be back in a few days. Just think about it."

"And if I say no?"

"Well, that is a bit of a gray area," said Foley. "I can't necessarily say what the ramifications would be in that case."

Tyker curled his fingers into the shape of a crude gun and pointed it at Henry. "Bang," he said with a grin. Henry's heart stopped for a moment.

"Oh, stop it," said Foley. "It's not like that. But I can't say for certain that the U.S. government would be one hundred percent thrilled at the idea of someone with your type of power running around utterly unchecked. Just consider it; that's all I ask. We can discuss more once I've hammered out the details." He rummaged through his coat pocket and produced a business card. It was a bit tattered, with one bent corner and what appeared to be a small coffee stain in the middle. He handed the card to Henry. "Give me a call if you have any questions or concerns in the meantime."

"Actually, I have a concern right now," said Henry. "Sure, maybe you guys are taking off. Maybe not. But now that you know who I am, am I going to be under surveillance? Like, am I going to be tracked and watched everywhere I go from now on?"

Tyker chortled. "Like hell," he said. "We're understaffed as it is, and with our department's budget looking the way it does, Foley here probably shouldn't even *be* on the payroll anymore. We don't have the resources to tail you twenty-four hours a day. Hell, it took us four damn days to find you in the first place, in a backwater Podunk town like this one. It's disgraceful."

"Just relax," said Foley with a sweep of his upturned palm. "We're not trying to make your life a living hell."

The trio was approaching the front entrance to St. Dante High, and several students were staring at them. Tyker had already turned and begun to walk away, a dark blot with a halo vanishing down the sidewalk. Foley gave Henry a light pat on the shoulder. "Be seeing you," he said softly, and he too was gone.

As Henry walked into the school, he ignored the gazes of his peers as he pored over Foley's business card. It was plain and stark, a white background with the sort of black type that looked as though it had been produced by some antique typewriter. It merely said "James Foley," and had a single phone number beneath that. No job title, no department identification, nothing official of any sort. It was almost reassuring; if the whole encounter had been some sort of sinister hoax, it seemed as though his companions would have at least tried harder to make their business cards convincing. Still, Henry flicked it into the bushes like a burnt-out cigarette.

"The hell with this," he muttered.

Henry took a few steps, then looked around him. As a smattering of his fellow students watched on, he walked back over to the bushes, picked up the tattered card, and stuffed it into his back pocket.

When twilight fell that evening, Henry was alone in the woods. As the shadows of trees grew longer around him like gnarled fingers, he practiced wielding the scythe. When he had first removed it from his lunchbox, he had been reluctant even to push the button and extend it; it made his skin crawl. But when he finally ripped off the metaphorical bandage and held the scythe in all its terrible glory, the creepiness abated in the wake of the sheer power radiating from the weapon. A grin seeped across Henry's face like blood through a towel as, for the first time since his thrashing at Vargas's hands, he actually felt powerful. Unstoppable.

The sense of might was hindered by the stark realization that Henry had no idea how to use the scythe effectively. Unlike a sword or a gun, this was an unintuitive and somewhat unwieldy weapon. The pointed tip allowed it to be used as a sort of spear, but frantic jabbing was clearly not using the scythe to its full potential. With some effort, Henry developed a graceful, if somewhat hesitant, slashing motion that could be useful for keeping Vargas at bay, if nothing else. As the last few rays of sunlight glinted off the curved blade, Henry could swear he felt the oxygen molecules in the air being vivisected with each pass of the scythe.

"Oh my God! What the hell is that?" someone behind Henry exclaimed.

Henry whirled around, his eyes wide, his breath trapped in his lungs. Doug was rapidly approaching, and though his features were darkened by the encroaching night, he was clearly shaking his head in apparent disbelief. Henry's mind reeled, neurons firing in a desperate attempt to explain away his peculiar weaponry without giving away all of his secrets.

"It, uh…it's a scythe," Henry choked out through his suddenly moisture-free mouth.

"I can see that," said Doug, leaning in to examine it. "The scythe of the future, apparently. Don't tell me you built this yourself. What, do you have super inventing powers now? Is this like Peter Parker inventing web shooters when he first became Spider-Man?"

"No, not at all. And don't touch. Be careful," Henry said, lightly swatting away Doug's hand, which had been steadily creeping toward the weapon. "It, um…it was…Vargas, uh, dropped it when we fought, I guess. I couldn't make anything like this."

"And you're just mentioning this now? It would seem to be fairly significant."

"I didn't even realize. Watch," said Henry. He hit the button, and the scythe folded up into it small, cylindrical form.

"This is what I looked like. I just figured it out by accident."

"You still should've called me and let me know," said Doug. "No sense in keeping things from me, Henry. The more I and the rest of us know, the more we might be able to help you out. Plus, this is really exciting."

"Yeah," said Henry with the most paltry of laughs. "I'm sorry about that. You're right, I should have told you. I guess I was just sort of embarrassed…I don't even hardly know how to use the damn thing."

"It's certainly not the sort of thing they teach us in P.E." said Doug. "Come on, let me hold it."

"Don't do it. It'd burn your hands off. The only reason I can do it is because of these gloves, and even then, it's hard to hold it for very long."

"So it's hot then? Like…what, a hot plate or something?"

"I don't even know if it's heat exactly," said Henry, scratching the back of his neck. "It's strange. It's not an easy sensation to describe, but it's really unpleasant. It's like a cross between heat, electricity, and really bad anxiety."

"That's so awesome," said Doug. "Well, let me put the gloves on and hold it then."

"No! No," said Henry, his heart rate spiking, "it's too unsafe. Even with the gloves on, I think my, ah, powers are the only reason I can withstand it. I'm sorry, but I don't want you to get hurt, so I can't."

"Aw, crap," said Doug, stuffing his hands in his pockets.

"Anyway," said Henry, "I'm trying to figure out how to use this thing in some way so that I at least don't look like a *complete* spaz. It doesn't do me much good if I can't even defend myself with it."

"And I'd imagine Vargas will probably be wanting it back. But hey, good for you," said Doug, slapping Henry on the back. "Ow. There might be some hope for you yet, if we can get this figured out."

"For sure, for sure. Anyway, we should probably be heading home before it gets too late. In a few minutes we won't even be able to see each other anymore."

"That's more of a loss for you than it is for me," said Doug.

"That's cute," said Henry.

As the boys walked home, Doug rambled enthusiastically about the scythe and Henry and Vargas and how, if the town didn't burn to the ground, their confrontation was going to be remembered as the greatest spectacle in St. Dante's history. Henry just sighed and mumbled a series of halfhearted affirmations. His eyes rarely left the ground.

Chapter Nine

The week flew by on wings of anxiety. Henry's nightmares intensified in scale and frequency, and his body grudgingly grew accustomed to bouts of brief, fitful sleep. On the plus side, his wounds were healing remarkably quickly, and much to the astonishment of his peers, he was more or less back to normal within a couple of days. Albert remarked that the swift healing must be another of Henry's new powers, which made as much sense as any other explanation. In any case, Henry was in good shape physically far sooner than he had anticipated. Mentally…that was another story.

Each afternoon, Henry made sure to spend an hour or so in the woods, grimly training by himself with the scythe, cutting leaves to ribbons in midair with increasing speed and precision. The bulk of his days, however, were spent with his family and friends; Henry realized that this could be the last week he ever had in their company, and budgeted his time accordingly. His parents, despite their initial concern over the injuries Henry had received from Vargas, seemingly suspected nothing was amiss, as they behaved no differently than usual. His father bemoaned his joblessness while brainstorming possible ways to make money off of Henry's talents, and his mother toiled ceaselessly to keep the family afloat and upbeat. Henry's grandmother, however, was sullen and aloof. She hardly ate, and whenever she spoke to Henry, her voice rose scarcely above a whisper and her eyes welled up with moisture. She even refrained from complaining about other people's driving for the first time anyone could recall. Henry figured she knew something about what was going on, but she never mentioned it directly, and Henry was certainly not going to bring up the subject.

Doug, Albert and Trent had decided amongst themselves that any displays of worry or sorrow were best kept in private, since they didn't want Henry to think that they doubted him, and even if this was going to be Henry's last week on this Earth, it would be best served in celebration rather than mourning. Doug described it as a week-long Dia de los Muertos, which sounded good to the boys despite the fact that none of them had ever celebrated the holiday in the first place.

"I've heard good things about it," said Doug.

"Me too," said Albert. "Or maybe I'm thinking of All Souls' Day."

"Or All Saints' Day," said Trent.

"Aren't they the same thing?" said Albert. No one was quite sure of the answer.

Wednesday night, two days before Vargas's promised return, Henry found his insomnia reaching previously unheard of levels, so he turned himself over to his newly operational Nintendo Entertainment System. He blazed through *Super Mario Bros.*, which still retained a decent challenge level despite being easier than Henry remembered from his previous play through nearly a decade ago. Henry and his family had been visiting his aunt in Nevada, and his teenage cousin was playing the family NES. Though quite dated even then, Henry's cousin explained that he appreciated the challenge of the classic games, and found them to be more fun than newer ones despite their lack of flashy graphics or complex sound capabilities. Henry was not certain that he agreed with that assessment, but he played along and got a tremendously entertaining couple of afternoons out of it.

Now, Mario's sprawling quest to rescue the kidnapped princess was a welcome respite from dark thoughts of Henry's looming fate. At the end of each world, Mario would face off with a massive, powerful enemy who was far too mighty to be defeated by Mario's normal methods of attack. Rather than engage in a futile direct physical confrontation, the key to overcoming his immense, fire-breathing nemesis was to guide Mario past him and hack down the bridge the beast stood upon with an axe conveniently located on the far side, thereby plunging the creature into a pool of lava and presumably disintegrating him into a charred husk. Henry's thoughts wandered back to Vargas, and he lamented the lack of bridges suspended over lava pools in the area. Mario didn't know how easy he had it.

At school, Denise Hargrove didn't have much to say to Henry anymore, and his awkward attempts at initiating conversation were met with glares that could charitably be described as icy. On the other hand, Roderick King III, despite his recent misfortunes, had plenty to say.

"You still here, Garrison?" he asked Henry one chilly morning. Roderick's omnipresent cadre of friends hung back much further than usual, nervously muttering amongst themselves and casting wary glances at Henry. "I thought your buddies would have hauled you off by now."

"And what buddies would those be?" said Henry.

"You know who I'm talking about. They must have found you by now," said Roderick. He held up his thumb and forefinger, just barely spaced apart. "They were this close already."

"Ah. The government guys," said Henry. "I should have figured you'd clue them in about me. You're just such a helpful guy, after all. Always walking old ladies across the street and all that."

"Just doing my civic duty. I'm not really comfortable having freaks run around in my hometown."

"Yes, and thanks for that, by the way. They actually were looking for me so that they could offer me a job. Very important, prestigious stuff. So *gracias* for having my back there, Rod. It means a lot to me that you would look out for my welfare like that."

"Why don't you take the job then? Take the job and just go away," said Roderick. Steam billowed from his mouth into the frosty air as he spat, "Trust me, you're not doing anybody any good here."

"And here I thought we were getting along so well," said Henry. "Well, no need for the torches and pitchforks, man. I might be out of here sooner than you think."

"I hope so," said Roderick. "And I bet Denise feels the same way."

"That's not the impression she gave me," said Henry. He wanted to say more, to verbally castrate Roderick with the fact that his girlfriend had asked Henry to the dance. But something held him back, some tiny voice that noted the difference between self-defense and cruelty, some intangible lasso that whirled Henry around and made him walk away. Roderick took a step after him, then stopped. As he removed a stick of gum from his coat pocket and chewed it with a series of wet, viscous smacks, he never took his eyes off Henry's form slowly becoming enveloped by the fog ahead.

"I still think you could totally kick his ass," one of his friends said.

"Oh, just shut up," snapped Roderick.

Thursday night, Doug suggested that Henry and the boys go out for what each of them silently feared would be their last big night out. The destination he suggested was a small Korean bar called Note on the east side of town that offered a particularly appealing combination: karaoke and an exceedingly lax policy in terms of serving alcohol to minors. The other boys were somewhat dubious about this idea. Albert was worried about getting grounded and forced to miss the Halloween dance, while Henry had no great desire for another uncomfortable run-in with Sheriff Porter. Trent actually thought it was a decent plan, but reveled in the opportunity to argue with Doug. In the end, Doug's depressingly realistic run-down of their alternatives sold the boys on taking their chances at Note. It certainly beat the food court at the mall or the formerly 24-hour Dante Donuts, now in ruins due to the recent monster attack.

Any paranoia ended up being unfounded, as the doorman, wearing sunglasses despite the lateness of the hour, lowered his shades at the sight of Henry and unleashed an indefinable ejaculation of glee somewhere between a squeal and a hoot. The doorman giddily explained that he had been downtown during the creature's rampage and, despite his better judgment, had neglected his personal safety in order to get a closer view of what was going on. He had seen Henry club the creature's cranium with the crane hook, but had been trying unsuccessfully to describe the scenario to his fellow bar dwellers. Now that the boy was physically in his presence, his story could finally be both verified and completed, and his gratitude was immense. Hurrying Henry and the others inside, the doorman stood up on a wobbly table and called for the attention of everyone in the bar. Albert blushed as all eyes turned toward the boys, and he mumbled a prayer for his freedom. The karaoke stopped momentarily, and the doorman regaled the Note patrons with a tastefully exaggerated account of the recent rampage while making sweeping gestures at Henry. Occasionally Henry would offer a nod or affirmation to keep the story going, but the doorman did the bulk of the heavy lifting, telling his story as if the gods themselves were in his presence. Upon his story's conclusion, laughter and mirth filled the room to swelling, and the handful of bar denizens swarmed around Henry with Cheshire smiles and offers of drinks on the house. Any chance that age verification might be a problem had gone right out the window.

Henry, for his part, delighted in the attention, shaking hands and retelling bits and pieces of the doorman's tale. Liquor and beer were poured in honor of St. Dante's savior, and in the blink of an eye Henry's table was laden with proffered booze.

"Do you think you guys might be able to help me out with getting these drank?" Henry said to Doug, Trent, and Albert. "I don't really want any alcohol; I have to be in top form tomorrow for my little date with destiny tomorrow."

"Destiny? I hear she's hot," said Trent.

"Fail," said Albert, shaking his head in disgust.

"Don't worry. We've got your back," said Doug, grabbing a rum and Coke and a glass of some very dark beer. "I mean, what are friends for, right?"

"Oh, not me," said Albert. "I don't, you know, do that. Drink, I mean. I'm here for the ambiance."

"It's just you and me, I guess," said Doug, waving his finger between himself and Trent. "We've gotta represent."

"Well, if I *have* to..." said Trent, sliding a beer toward himself.

Within an hour, Doug was feeling no pain. He stood on stage, his shirt unbuttoned to reveal the decreasingly white undershirt beneath, belting out a shrill version of Celine Dion's "My Heart Will Go On." One hand held the microphone, the other a beer, more of which was ending up on the stage than in his mouth. As the small crowd cheered him, Doug executed some bizarre stomping dance moves and come-hither hand gestures. Trent filmed the woozy performance on his camera phone, chuckling wickedly.

"Now I see why there are laws regarding the drinking age," said Henry.

"I don't know," said Albert. "You've seen some of these other guys. I don't think it gets much better when you're older."

"In a way, though, it can't really get much better than this," said Henry as Doug botched an attempt to slide across the stage on his knees, instead falling over onto his side. "I think this is how Doug would want to be remembered."

After a few moments of Doug's caterwauling, Albert leaned in to Henry and said, "Not to ruin the mood, and stop me if you don't want to discuss this right now, but have you thought of any other weaknesses that this Vargas guy has? We have his head, maybe, and then this weapon of his that you got a hold of, but did you come up with anything else?"

Without taking his eyes off Doug, Henry said, "Maybe. I don't know. I was thinking last night about how my biggest advantage is probably the fact that this is my home turf. I must know the area way better than Vargas does, so that's something. I just don't know how to exploit that, exactly."

"You could set up traps or something," said Albert. "Surprise him. It could work."

"Yeah, but think about the caliber of opponent this guy is. I couldn't even scratch him with a full-on assault. And sure, he won't surprise me as much this time, but what kind of trap could I set that would even make a dent in someone like that? It's not like I have access to explosives or anything."

"Hmmm…that's a good point," said Albert. He sighed. "Too bad this isn't like *Home Alone*. That kid had traps for days."

"Oh, come on. The burglars in that movie were like immortal," said Henry. "He threw a brick at the one guy's head from the roof of a building and the guy walked away from it." He took a sip from the tonic water he was nursing. "I think I'd rather go up against Vargas than those guys."

"See? There you go," said Albert. "Silver lining."

Henry looked over to Trent, who was mesmerized by Doug's performance. He thought he could see a glimmer of light reflecting off something on Trent's cheek.

"Are those…tears?" gasped Henry.

"Hay fever," Trent grunted, with a soggy sniffle.

Doug's song ended, and he wandered over to the boys' table and spun into his seat. "Top that one, Ace," he said to Henry.

"I intend to. Excuse me," he said, glancing up at the

glowing monitor that flashed his name. "I believe that means it's my turn."

As Henry walked up an seized the microphone, Doug turned to Albert. "Do you have any idea what he's going to sing?" Albert shook his head. Trent took a sip of beer and blew his nose on a napkin.

Henry turned his back to the audience, so that the "HENRY GARRISON" logo on the back of his sweatshirt was clearly visible. He rolled the microphone lightly between his fingers as the bar patrons chanted his name. The pale stage lights captured Henry's pose, and a hush fell over the room. A few quick drumbeats carried through the speakers, and then the room was flooded with the seductive wail of a saxophone.

"Dear God," said Trent. "Not 'Careless Whisper.'"

"What is this? How does he even know this song?" said Albert. He turned to Trent. "And how do you?"

"My mom always liked to listen to light rock in the car," said Trent.

Henry whirled around seconds before the vocals came in,

and clutched the microphone near his mouth. His eyes clamped shut and he crouched like a jaguar about to pounce as he sang the lyrics to the George Michael classic in a breathy coo. His free hand swept grandly, clutching for something ephemeral as the song built to a crescendo and the coo blossomed into a wail of intensely joyful heartache. The bar's spinning light display cavorted all about Henry's crooning form, a cascade of whirring autumnal hues. For one glorious moment, Henry's anxiety melted away like snow cast into the sun, replaced wholly by the bliss of the performance. At the end of the performance, Henry fell to his knees, bowing his head as the small room swelled with whoops and shrieks of approval.

"You bastard," said Doug as Henry returned to his seat. His words oozed out in a barely intelligible verbal slime. "I can't believe you upstaged me like that. Good one."

"Are those tears?" Trent queried, looking at Henry's slightly reflective cheeks and quivering lower lip.

"Hay fever," Henry said. He sniffed. Albert handed him a tissue.

Faint gray light had barely begun to seep through Henry's window when his alarm went off. The fated morning had arrived, and as his eyelids snapped back, Henry felt an unusual sense of calm. He was alive, and in his bedroom. Moreover, for the first time in days he felt rested; relaxed, even. So far, so good.

As Henry descended the stairs, he was greeted by the pop and hiss of sizzling bacon and the heartbreaking realization that this might well be the last time he ever saw his family. His mother was frantic, drifting between tasks like a domesticated ghost, and his father glumly poked at a cooling plate of scrambled eggs without raising his gaze from the tabletop, but for once Henry found their behavior comforting rather than off-putting. He wore his best smile impersonation as he sat down for breakfast.

"I'm sorry, I think the toast is burnt," his mother said, placing a plate before Henry as she scooted by the table to check on the dryer in the garage.

"It's fine. I'm sure it'll be great," said Henry, but his only response was the muffled slam of the garage door. He looked across the table at his father, half expecting a pigeon to land on the motionless man and wondering if such an event would even provoke a reaction. "Thank God it's Friday, huh?" Henry said, reaching into his bag of clichés.

"Makes no difference to me," his father muttered. "Every day is my Friday. Or Saturday, I guess."

"You never know," said Henry through a mouthful of pork. "Something good might happen today."

"You figured out how to make any money yet off of those powers of yours?"

"Well, no."

"Then I doubt anything good will happen today," said Henry's father. He sighed, then looked Henry in the eye. "But hey, you're right. You never know."

"Where's grandma this morning?"

"She isn't feeling well. Wants to be left alone, she said," said Henry's mother, emerging from the garage with a basket of laundry. "Probably should just let her sleep."

"Probably," said Henry. This was no good. He wanted to at least say goodbye to his grandmother before he went to school, given the circumstances. But he wasn't sure if he had it in him to shake a sick old woman awake. Not this early in the morning, anyway.

"You should get a move on," Henry's mother said. "You're running late."

Was it time already? Had the morning flown by so quickly? The pre-school period of the day usually ended fairly swiftly, but still…

"Did you hear me?" his mother said.

"Yeah, yeah," said Henry. "Sorry. Just thinking about tonight. I don't think I'm coming straight home from school tonight…Albert is going to the Halloween dance tonight and he's kind of nervous, so I think me and the guys are going to go to show our support."

"You're going to a dance with a bunch of guys?" said Henry's father, his eyes still focused on his eggs. "I guess I shouldn't be surprised."

"Anyway, I won't be home until late, probably. So, you know. Just so you're not worried about me or anything, that's where

I'll be."

"OK. Well, have fun, dear," Henry's mother said. Henry looked at her, and his eyes suddenly filled with tears. Blinking them away like unwelcome gnats, he embraced his mother with a firm hug. She squeaked in surprise, then furrowed her brow as she hugged him back. Both she and Henry's father watched Henry quizzically.

"What was that all about?" Henry's mother said.

"Nothing," said Henry, his eyes widening with exaggerated blinks. "I just don't do that enough."

"Weirder by the second," Henry's father grumbled.

"Goodbye, guys," Henry said as he whirled to face the door. He refused to look behind him as he marched toward the big tan rectangle that separated himself from his destiny. Just as he laid his hand upon the doorknob, he felt his grandmother's softly, mildly clammy grip upon his left shoulder. Where did she come from?

"Henry," she said, turning him gently to face her. Her visage was unbearably sad, each line and crease on her face dipping into a chasm of sorrow. Henry went numb at this sudden exposure to inconceivable grief, and his arms drifted up of their own will, slow and light as dead leaves in the wind, embracing the old woman.

"I never should have let you go into the attic," she whispered in a tone so soft that Henry was unsure of whether or not the dialogue had been his imagination. "Goodbye, my dear boy." And with that, she departed as quickly as she came, shuffling across the room like a wind-up toy.

"Well, this sure is an emotional morning," chortled Henry's father. "What're you, going off to war or something?"

Henry paused. "No, just going to school. Have a good one."

As Henry approached the high school, he could see Doug, Albert and Trent waiting for him out in front. Albert seemed anxious, and Trent had obvious bags under his eyes, but Doug was clearly the worst for wear. Sporting huge sunglasses with lenses black as tar that Henry had never seen before, Doug coughed and patted Henry on the back when his friend approached. He smelled like mouthwash and, somewhere underneath that medicinal aroma, something sickly sweet that was hard to pinpoint. Making an effort to do so would be a nauseating task, so Henry chose to ignore it to the best of his abilities.

"If you ever needed proof that I love ya, man," said Doug in a hoarse bellow, "the fact that I showed up at school today should be all you need. Nobody else could have dragged me out of bed this morning."

"Not feeling so hot?" said Henry.

"Like grim death," said Doug.

"Still better than your singing," said Trent.

"Oh, don't even start with me, Waterworks," snapped Doug. "I doubt you're feeling much better, anyway. What were we thinking?"

"This is all so stressful," said Albert. "I couldn't sleep last night."

"It's nice of you to be worried, but it'll be fine," said Henry. "I'll make it through this."

"Huh? I was talking about the Halloween dance tonight. I'm so nervous…I've never done anything like this before. Of course,

I'm worried about you too."

"Well that's positively heart-warming," sighed Henry. "You'll be fine tonight. Really. I'm sure Jenny likes you; otherwise, why would she have agreed to go with you? It'll be awesome."

"I hope you," said Albert. "I wish you could go. It might help my nerves."

"Well, inter-dimensional kidnapping does have a way of mucking up one's schedule," said Henry. "Next time, I'll try not to schedule it on the same night as a major social event."

"God, I want a burrito right now," moaned Doug.

"How about you, Henry? Did you sleep OK?" said Trent. "Probably not. Hell, I didn't even sleep well, and I have relatively little to worry about."

"You know, I actually slept alright," said Henry. "Don't ask me why. Maybe I was so exhausted that I couldn't help it. Maybe I've just given in to the whole situation, and settled into acceptance to the point where I'm content just letting the chips fall where they may."

"Or maybe you're just so confident in yourself that you're

not even sweating this anymore," said Doug.

"Maybe."

"So what's the plan? When's your boy showing up?" said Trent.

"Yeah, I've gotta make sure I get good seats," said Doug.

"That's an excellent question. I really don't know. It depends on how literal he was being when he told me I had eight days and not a moment more. He might show up at the eight-day mark, to the second. Or he might just bust into one of my classes and knock my head off before I can get out of the damn single-piece desk and chair ensemble the school forces us to endure. We'll find out."

"For what it's worth, I hope it's not the second one," said Albert.

"Thanks. Now, as for what Doug was saying…" Henry said. He scanned his friends' faces, seeing expressions of exhaustion and anxiety, betrayed by an intense glint of excitement in their eyes (he had to assume in the case of Doug's eyes). Henry's impending showdown with Vargas was imposing, to be sure; it also happened to be more hotly anticipated than the Super Bowl, the World Series, and Quarter Hot Dog Night combined, if only for these boys. This wasn't going to be pleasant.

"About getting good seats…I would honestly prefer if you guys just sort of…stay away from this whole thing. The fight. It's going to get ugly, and I don't want any of you getting hurt."

"You've got to be kidding," said Doug. "I'm not missing this. When else am I going to get to see a super powered smackdown live and in person?"

"Never," said Henry. "Because you guys are not going to be there. It's too dangerous."

"He probably has a point," said Albert.

"Forget it!" said Trent. "There's no way we're not going to be there. We're your backup…you're crazy if you think we're letting you do this alone."

"You can't be my backup. Actually, you'll just be a liability."

"Gee, thanks," said Trent.

"That's messed up, dude," said Doug.

"OK, I didn't mean that the way it sounded," said Henry.

He wrung his hands and glanced at the worn leather gloves, then back to his friends. "But Vargas doesn't strike me as the type to screw around. There could be serious collateral damage; in fact, I'd bet on it. Plus, if things get hairy, he might end up trying to take one of your guys hostage, and I just can't have that. I've been trying to figure out his weaknesses all week…I'd have to think he might have at least considered mine."

"So we're a weakness now?" said Trent.

"I'm just saying that there's potential for disaster if you guys are there. I appreciate your support, I really do. I'm just…I just worry about what could happen, and I won't put you guys in harm's way. Please, go to the dance with Albert or something. He needs you guys to be there with him tonight…you see how nervous he is. I'll be fine by myself. Really."

"I'm not going to no stupid dance," said Trent. "No offense, Albert."

"None taken," Albert said.

"I can't believe you're asking me to not have your back when you go up against Vargas," said Doug.

"I'm not asking you. I'm *telling* you," said Henry. He looked Doug directly in the sunglass-shielded eyes. "I can deal with my blood being spilled. Not yours."

"This is ridiculous," said Trent.

"It makes sense, though," said Albert. "What could you guys really do? You'd just be getting in the way."

"Oh, shut up," said Trent. "You weren't going anyway. What do you care?"

"Alright, knock it off," said Henry. "I gotta get to class. If you guys are going to be mad about this, then fine. Just please do this for me. And you can yell at me about this when it's all over."

"Oh, don't worry," said Doug. "We will, I assure you."

Walking into Mrs. Tegg's class, Henry gazed at Denise Hargrove's already seated form, her hair and makeup impeccable as usual. As he slid into his uncomfortable little desk, he gave her a slight nod and grunted a sheepish greeting. Her rebuttal was a silent, positively arctic stare.

"Hey, I've got good news for you," said Henry, leaning in to her. "If you're lucky, you may never have to see me again after today."

"Doubt I'd be that lucky," she said, shrugging, and stared straight ahead, as Mrs. Tegg gave a cough to signal her intention of beginning the day's lesson.

"We'll see," Henry whispered, and then slumped back into his chair.

The rest of the day was tense but uneventful. Henry jumped at every movement his peripheral vision picked up, but the day was almost shockingly ordinary. Classes proceeded ponderously, teachers lecturing in monotonous futility as Henry drummed his fingers on his desktop in anxious rhythm. Lunch was a solemn affair. Trent and Doug bristled at Henry's attempts at levity as Albert perspired heavily on account of his ceaseless worrying about the forthcoming dance, then perspired more with concern over his excessive perspiration and its possible effects on his appearance and odor. Henry was all too happy to discuss the dance with Albert, though he seemed the only one. As lunchtime ended, Henry headed off to his final classes while telling his friends he would see them later. He wasn't entirely certain he was being honest.

When his last class of the day ended, Henry wasted no time in exiting campus and headed off toward the woods. Dried orange and brown leaves crackled like live wires beneath him as he walked, and the vacant grins of freshly carved jack-o-lanterns mocked him from beige porches festooned with fake spider webs and gangling plastic skeletons. Henry swung his empty lunch box by his side in an exaggerated arc, a meager distraction from the jaws of fate which slowly, invisibly closed around Henry. The autumn wind whispered vague innuendoes as it slipped around Henry, through the tall trees ahead, and into oblivion. As the sun hovered barely above the treetops like a colossal will-o-the-wisp, the serenity of the afternoon resonated in Henry's head like a dirge.

The entire world froze, save one solitary element. Vargas's hulking form emerged from the woods, a phantom that swept, smooth yet unspeakably firm, right into Henry's path. Silhouetted in shade cast off by the vanishing sun behind him, Vargas looked exactly as he had eight days prior. In fact, were it not for the general cleanliness of his appearance, Henry might have figured that Vargas had in fact been simply waiting in the bushes since their last encounter. His mouth was a perfectly thin, straight horizontal line, but his eyes blazed with something primal. Whether it was excitement or annoyance was mystifying but ultimately irrelevant; the raw intensity of Vargas's gaze was such that all the blood in Henry's head practically evaporated.

"I believe it is the agreed upon time. I trust you have made your arrangements and are prepared to go," said Vargas. He stood unmoving, but he took sight of Henry's lunchbox. "You have certainly chosen an oddly small way to transport your belongings."

"Yeah, about that…" Henry stammered. Just breathe, he told himself. Breathe, stay conscious, stay in control of your bladder. You've got this. "I think I've reconsidered."

"Oh?" said Vargas. "Reconsidered? I must say, I find that very disappointing. Though not entirely surprising."

"So you're not surprised. That's good. Then this won't have to be all awkward." Henry had to slacken his grip on his lunchbox, as he felt the handle beginning to give from the sheer force being unthinkingly applied.

"I am unsurprised. That does not mean I am accepting."

"I guess I'll take what I can get."

"Must we really go through this all again?" said Vargas. He raised his right hand and spoke some words in a voice somewhere between whisper and auditory hallucination. The hand began to glow a deep orange, complementing the slowly dying daylight. "It really makes no sense. Why endure needless suffering? You will end up in my company regardless of your course of action."

A solitary click shattered the conversation. Cold steel pressed up against the point where Vargas's skull met his spine. He remained still, but his pupils snapped to the left.

"He's not going anywhere," said Tom Tyker, his forefinger caressing the trigger of his Glock.

Chapter Ten

Henry watched warily as Tyker's gun dug into the back of Vargas's neck. Pale orange late afternoon light washed over the scene, and not a single leaf so much as trembled. For a situation involving firearms and a super powered being from another dimension, it was a surprisingly tranquil moment.

"I take this to mean that there is no chance of you honoring our previous agreement, then?" said Vargas, his attention shifting from Tyker back to Henry.

"What can I say?" said Henry. "Something about being forced into servitude by an unknown entity kind of rubs me the wrong way."

"It does not matter. You will still come with me, one way or another."

"No one is going anywhere," said Foley. He emerged from the woods lethargically, his gun aimed directly at Vargas's face.

"The boy is under our protection."

"You must be joking. *You* are protecting *him*?" said Vargas, nodding slightly at Henry.

"Shut it, jackhole," said Tyker. "I'm not in the mood for small talk."

"I am just making a point," said Vargas. He looked into Henry's eyes. "They are not like you. They do not have your strength. You must be very desperate to go to men such as these for help, for I do not see what they can do that you cannot."

"You'd be surprised," said Tyker.

"Perhaps I would," mused Vargas. "But I am usually a good judge of these things."

"Look, that's it," said Henry. He took half a step toward Vargas. "Say what you want; you're the one with a gun to your head. And this guy will shoot, believe me. You should just chalk this up as a loss and go back to wherever you came from."

"Should I," said Vargas. He began to mumble something under his breath.

"I thought I told you to shut it," said Tyker. He shifted his weight to dig the muzzle of the gun deeper into Vargas's flesh. He then lost his balance and pitched forward as Vargas vanished.

"What the hell?" said Henry.

"Great," said Tyker, glancing around nervously. A leaf fluttered down and tapped the tip of his nose. "Looks like we've got a-" Tyker's chin nearly hit his knees as a massive amount of force connected with his stomach. Before he could hit the ground, another blow found his jaw, sending him spinning to earth. With a tiny gurgle, he collapsed to a fetal position on the grass.

Foley fired a single round, and Vargas's fleeting image vanished again. The forest was still. "This may be a bit more challenging than we had hoped," Foley said, mopping his brow with his free hand.

"Well, jeez, I never knew he could teleport!" said Henry.

"And how did you think he traveled between his dimension and ours, then? The bus?"

"No, I just figured it was…something different? A machine or a portal, maybe? I don't know how this stuff works."

"And you may be right," said Foley. His eyes ceaselessly

roved over their surroundings. "He might just be capable of bursts of extreme speed. But either way, I'm not exactly thrilled with the direction this is heading."

"What about him?" Henry said, pointing at Tyker's crumpled form.

"He seems to still be alive," said Foley, kneeling by Tyker and taking his pulse at the neck. "Which is fortunate; I'd bet this guy could swat him like a fly without breaking a sweat. Actually, it might have taken more effort for him *not* to kill Tom."

"That's good, at least," stammered Henry. "Where do you think he went?"

"Look," said Foley, "you should be thrilled that we even made it out here, given that you didn't call us about this until this morning. If you expected us to have some dossier full of secret intelligence info on this guy for you, then you've got another thing coming."

"But I thought you-"

"There's a reason we pursued you, Mr. Garrison. We simply aren't well-equipped to handle these extreme cases by ourselves.

Given a bit more warning, sure, we would have a more effective game plan, but what did you really expect us to do?"

"I don't know. Help me out, I guess," said Henry. "I'm not of much use to you guys if I'm trapped in another dimension."

"So you're saying that if you can get out of this, you're amenable to working with us?"

"I'll think about it," said Henry. His head whipped around as he thought he heard a noise coming from the trees.

"We're not out here putting our asses on the line for you to think about it," hissed Foley. "Who do you think you are?"

"Enough." The deep voice fell upon Henry and Foley like a murky, chilling fog. "Your petty arguments will have to be put on indefinite hold."

Vargas appeared in front of Foley, who instinctively raised his firearm. "Let me show you something I think you may find fascinating," said Vargas. "Aim that at my chest and fire."

Without a moment's hesitation, Foley did as he was told. Vargas let slip a fragment of a sound that may have been a grunt, or perhaps a chuckle. The bullet fell, molten hot, to the ground.

Vargas's clothing was unscathed.

"How did you do that?" said Foley. "Magic?"

"Magic? No need for that," said Vargas. "My people's capacity for lightweight armor technology is truly marvelous, is it not?"

"Interesting," said Foley, swinging his gun upwards. "So that means your head-"

Foley screamed as Vargas chopped him squarely in the right shoulder. His arm fell limp but his side, and his gun fell pathetically to the grass with a muffled thump. Foley squinted up at his assailant through bleary eyes. Vargas raised his hand once more.

The punch landed with an ugly thud. With a rumbling groan, Vargas pitched forward. His knees buckled, but he caught himself before his fall became irreversible and, clutching the back of his head, he turned around with bared teeth. Henry, his fist still clenched from the punch, stood there with eyes narrowed, breathing heavily.

"That was a very dishonorable attack," growled Vargas.

"I do what I gotta do," said Henry. "I'd say the deck is

sufficiently stacked against me that I'm not gonna lose any sleep over it."

"That philosophy will prove useful in my world," said Vargas. "But it will not be enough for you now."

"We'll see," said Henry. Scarcely had the words escaped his mouth when Vargas's fist flew at him. To his own surprise, Henry dodged capably, and responded with a solid knee to Vargas's stomach. Vargas pushed him away, but staggered a bit.

"Not bad. You are progressing," said Vargas. He lunged again, launching a visceral attack that snapped Henry into purely defensive mode. Henry threw up his hands before his face and tried to deflect the flurry of fists that flew at his face like five-fingered pistons. Then, planting his feet firmly into the ground, he launched himself backwards. A tiny explosion, a crunchy pop, occupied Henry's former position as he landed a few feet away. He steadied himself just in time to see the neon-green shards of his former lunchbox settle gently on the ground like extremely tacky snow. He had forgotten he was even carrying it.

"You monster!" he roared. "I can't believe it!"

"Is that really what you choose to concern yourself with at this point?" said Vargas. "Silly trinkets?"

"Trinkets?" Henry fumed. "I paid good money for that thing! That was a genuine European edition L.E.B.S. fan club lunchbox!" He dug into the right-hand pocket of his sweatshirt. "Now you've really gone and pissed me off."

Vargas eyed him quizzically as Henry removed the metal cylinder from his pocket. Glowering, he clicked the button with his thumb and felt an electric vibration surge through him as the scythe extended. For the first time, the unearthly power flowing through the ghastly weapon was downright comforting.

"You might be stronger than me," said Henry. "But I can kill you with this thing if I have to."

"What is that? Where did you get it?" said Vargas. "Your people could not have possibly created something like that."

"How do you know?" said Henry. "We created the atomic bomb, after all. Not that I'm particularly proud of that, exactly, but we did."

"You know what I am talking about," said Vargas. "The

magical energy coming off of that weapon is breathtaking. And though it is very similar to the energy you exude, there is simply no possibility that you created that weapon yourself. Certainly not with the level of intelligence you have displayed. Naturally, I am curious as to its origins."

"If you're so interested in it," Henry said, glancing at the curved blade by his side, "how about we make a deal: you leave me alone, and go back to wherever you came from without causing me any more problems, and I'll give you this scythe. Period, end of story. Everybody's happy. How about it?"

"Or I could simply beat you into submission, then take both you and the scythe with me when I return to my homeland," said Vargas. "I think I will choose that option."

"Why do you have to make everything so difficult?" moaned Henry.

"Why do *you*?"

"Fine," said Henry. "If that's how you want it. Don't say I didn't give you a way out."

"Absolutely."

Henry rushed at Vargas, gripping the scythe with skin-rupturing force as Vargas stood ready to defend himself. When he got within striking distance, though, Henry froze up. What exactly was he going to do? It was one thing to slice leaves in half, but a human being? How could he penetrate Vargas's armor without flat-out killing him?

Vargas, cognizant of Henry's hesitation, elbowed him in the face and kneed him in the gut. He then grabbed the hood of Henry's sweatshirt, lifted the boy from the ground, and threw him, gasping, through a tree. The top half collapsed onto Henry with a shimmering crash.

"This is feeling very familiar," said Vargas. He walked over to the heap of ruined tree, his boots crunching dried orange leaves into powder. "Surely you-"

Henry leapt out of the pile of leaves and branches and caught Vargas's neck in the crook of his right arm, knocking Vargas backwards off his feet. Squeezing as he landed, Henry used his forward momentum and hurled Vargas, with all the force he could muster, into the depths of the forest. Tree trunks shattered, pulverized, as the wizard's body vanished into the woods amidst a cacophony of cracks and crashing.

"Jerk," said Henry. He watched a murder of crows fly overhead, flitting black specters panicked by the commotion. Their caws of terror echoed through the rapidly darkening sky. Henry then turned to Foley, who was huddled against an elm tree, wheezing as he clutched his shattered shoulder. "I'm sorry I dragged you into this," Henry said.

Foley looked up with red-rimmed eyes. "Sorry we couldn't be of more help," he said.

Henry nodded, then plunged into the woods. One way or another, he was ending this tonight.

Though Henry was hardly the detective type, following Vargas's flight path could not have been much easier; the line of ruptured tree trunks was like a path of breadcrumbs leading Henry, however tentatively, to his target. Grumbling about his sore face (his head was still swimming a bit from Vargas's savage elbow), he trekked into the dusky forest. The destruction went further back than Henry had imagined, with several dozen trees feeling the unplanned wrath of Vargas's body. Though nervous, Henry could not stifle a bemused, wry grin at his own strength.

Finally, Henry found an oak tree with a trunk that, though scuffed and missing some bark, was still largely intact. With the woods behind it looking unscathed, Henry was forced to assume that this was the point at which Vargas had finally stopped. The fact that Vargas was not actually there was a bit troubling, however, and Henry squatted down before the damaged oak in order to take a closer look.

Eerie laughter, like the chuckle of an arrogant poltergeist, broke the forest's silence. Henry jolted to attention, heaving his body upwards reflexively. A cursory scan of the area revealed that Vargas was nowhere to be seen, but he most definitely could be heard. The fact that the late afternoon light was rapidly waning dawned on Henry, as he began to wonder how much moonlight might seep through the tree branches to save him from battling a wizard in inky darkness. Fortunately, it was looking like a clear night, despite the chill in the air. The first few stars of the evening winked at Henry, mocking his potential doom from their lofty perch light years away.

The laughter was short-lived, but gave Henry an idea of which direction his opponent had headed. With quivering legs dragging concrete feet through the crackling piles of earth-toned leaves, Henry sought the source of the chuckle. As it turns out, he did not have to go far.

Henry entered a clearing and was greeted by the babbling La Estigia River. On the opposite side stood Vargas, his arms crossed. Droplets of water glistened on his face, which was marred by an ugly gash across his forehead. Despite this, Vargas's mouth was ever so slightly upturned in a faint grin that oozed malice.

"I am impressed," he mused. "You have proven just as aggressive as before, perhaps even more so. But much less reckless. You have been preparing yourself, just as I hoped. You have a ways to go, as you shall see, but you have definitely displayed the sort of potential I had thought you would. When this is over with, you will be a fine warrior."

"I think I'm doing pretty damn well for myself as it is," said

Henry. "But if you wanna see a warrior, I'll show you a warrior." With a swift motion, the scythe extended in his right hand.

"Ah, the weapon again," said Vargas. "It really is quite marvelous. I shall enjoy wielding it once I have pried it from your battered, bloody fingers."

"You really should consider using contractions every once in a while," said Henry. "It'd make you sound much less…talky."

"What?" said Vargas.

"Just some grammatical humor," said Henry. "Probably inappropriate right now."

"You are a strange one," said Vargas. "But no matter. I suppose it is time we ended this nonsense." He began an indecipherable chant and made a strange gesture with his left hand.

The earth beneath Henry's feet erupted with flame, hurling him forward into the river with a whooshing splash. He had reflexively thrown his hands up in his face to defend himself, and thus had no mystical buffer between himself and the river. Frigid water rushed into his open mouth for a moment before he forced his head above the surface of the water, gasping. His eyes bleary, he could just barely make out Vargas's upraised hands before the water around him rose unnaturally. A thick, whirling column of water ascended twisting from the river, a terrible arm with rainbow veins. One choked whimper escaped Henry's throat before the piston of water slammed into the side of his head like a shimmering battering ram. Stunned, Henry slipped once again beneath the gurgling river. The chill of the water kept him conscious, but his thoughts were a discombobulated mess. His cheeks puffed out in a groggy wheeze, Henry planted his feet at the bottom of the river, fought to steady himself against the current, and jumped with all the strength he could muster. He broke the surface of the water and landed on the bank of the river, but his relief was short-lived as he tripped on the charred clumps of clay that Vargas's fireball had scattered about. He landed on his backside with a grunt that was equal parts frustration and embarrassment.

"How utterly ridiculous," said Vargas.

"Yeah, well," said Henry, attempting to muster up some machismo, "why don't you come over here and tell me how ridiculous I am?"

"That weapon you have there is potentially very dangerous," said Vargas. "Why would I get anywhere near you while you wield it?"

"I don't know. Honor or something?" said Henry, rising to his feet and dusting himself off.

"There is an immense difference between honor and stupidity, and I do not intend to fall prey to the latter."

"How wonderful for you."

"Instead, I will just use the weapons at my disposal," said Vargas. Henry could see the beginnings of another gesture, and just barely avoided another fiery explosion.

"Kind of a one-trick pony, aren't you?" Henry said. "Punches, kicks and fireballs. You're like an albino Ryu from *Street Fighter*."

"I do not think I have ever heard anyone spout as much nonsense as you do," said Vargas.

"If I'm getting on your nerves, you can always just leave me alone. My feelings won't get hurt or anything."

"Your attempts at levity are-" said Vargas. He was

interrupted by Henry, who charged at him, leaping the river entirely and slashing at his chest with the scythe. Vargas was able to just barely avoid the blade, which rent the air about him with a caustic whistle. He was likewise able to catch Henry's incoming left fist in the palm of his right hand by sheer instinct, but he was just off balance enough to allow Henry to successfully head butt him in the face. Vargas staggered back a few steps, snarling curses.

"You're right," Henry said. "I'll shut up now."

"So how the hell are we supposed to find him?" said Trent, shoving aside a leafy branch that he hoped was not poison oak. "They could be anywhere out here."

"OK, granted, that's true," said Doug, turning and inadvertently casting the flashlight's pale beam into Trent's eyes. "But how hard could it really be to find two superheroes fighting each other? I would imagine there must be at the very least some significant noise involved."

"I don't know that you could classify this Vargas guy as a superhero," said Doug, blinking away an army of dark gray pulsating floaters. "Or even Henry, really, if you really think about it."

"Hey, he managed to prevent a huge, terrifying monster from destroying downtown, so I think he counts as a superhero," said Doug. "Wow, that sounds really stupid when I say it out loud."

"I guess," said Trent. "I'm just kind of pissed about the whole 'you-can't-come-watch-me-have-an-awesome-fight' thing."

"He's just trying to do what he thinks is right," said Doug, brushing aside a particularly thorny branch. "He's totally wrong, of course, but he's trying."

"Don't you start in with that crap. I don't need to hear anymore about how we should be protected, and it's for our own good, and all that."

"Well, given our current course of action, I'd say it's pretty clear what we think of that advice."

"Crystal. Now if only we could just find that stupid idiot, we wouldn't have to be out here groping around in the dark."

"Do me a favor and keep the groping to yourself," said Doug.

"Screw you," said Trent. "Why don't you sing me some more Celine Dion?"

"Shhh," said Doug, raising his index finger to his lips. "Did you hear that?"

"I didn't hear anything. What was it?"

"I don't know."

Doug's words were met with a response in the form of the sort of crackling, swishing noises that indicated something was coming at the boys through the trees. It was low and staggered, but it was growing louder.

"That's definitely somebody coming," whispered Doug. "So here's the question: do we want them to find us?"

"What do you mean? Whoever it is, is coming right at us. Obviously they know where we are."

"For right now, yeah. But we don't have to make it easy on them. If we turn off the flashlight, it'll be a lot harder for them to find us."

"Wait, wait...you're suggesting we go running around in the dark-ass woods with no light whatsoever while some unknown being comes looking for us?"

"I'm not exactly suggesting it. I'm just offering it up as an option, that's all."

The swishing and crackling stopped. A shadowy figure loomed between the trees, coughing as it cast the beam of its own flashlight squarely onto Doug and Trent. The boys froze in place, their breath caught in their throats, their pupils dilated.

"We probably should have sped up that conversation a tad," Doug rasped.

"Evening, boys," said the gruff voice of Sheriff Porter as he emerged from the darkness. His eyes were underscored by a deep blackness cast backwards from the flashlight, making some fairly obvious bags even more unflattering. A faint glow from the badge on his breast gave his form a slight definition, yet even obscured and fatigued, Porter carried an unmistakable air of authority. His tone indicated what was, at best, irritation. "What are you two doing out here tonight? Got some Halloween pranks in mind? Because I would most certainly advise against that, if indeed that is what you happen to be planning."

"Pranks? Like what?" said Doug. "What kind of mischief-that's the kind of thing you would say, right? Mischief?-could we be getting into out here? There's not even anyone else around."

"Hmmm. I don't know. Vandalism, maybe. Arson."

"Arson? What, do you think we're out here to burn the forest down or something? Why would we ever do a thing like that?"

"I can't claim to understand why you kids do the things you do," said Porter dryly, "but nothing surprises me anymore. Sometimes I think the only reason you behave the way you do is to make my job harder. Lord knows I can't figure out any other explanation."

"With all due respect, sir," said Doug, "we have no desire to make your job any harder than it already is. Although I can't really imagine what you do around here most of the time, anyways."

"Oh my God, Doug," groaned Trent. "Are you trying to get us-"

"I suppose you think that's funny," snarled Porter. He marched right up to Doug and set his face so close that Doug could feel tiny flecks of spittle when Porter said, "You know, I've got a half-wrecked downtown area to clean up. I've got citizens having massive panic attacks because they think their quiet little world is going to hell in a hand basket, and the last thing I need is some punk kid telling me that I've just been resting on my laurels. And I have your little friend Henry to thank for this mess and the corresponding spike in my blood pressure. Where is he at tonight, anyway?"

"We don't know," said Trent quickly. "We were actually looking for him ourselves."

"Oh, so he *is* out here somewhere?"

"Maybe, maybe not," said Doug. "We thought he might be, but we haven't found him."

"Well, I got a call about some disturbance out here, so I wouldn't be surprised in the least if he's somehow involved. In fact, I'd bet dollars to donuts that he is quite heavily involved in whatever chicanery is going on. Unless, of course, the disturbance has something to do with you boys."

"Oh, no. Not us," said Trent. "We haven't seen or heard

anything weird out here. Well, until you scared the crap out of us a few minutes ago. That was weird. Or at least stressful."

"Yeah, it's been quiet out here, as far as we've seen," said Doug. "No ghosts, no goblins, not even any Jehovah's Witnesses. Just us and the squirrels."

"Well, I would suggest you boys go home. Isn't your school having a dance tonight? You should go to that. Or put on a couple of dresses and go Trick-or-Treating as the Doublemint twins. I don't care. Just get out of the woods, will you? I'm feeling particularly stressed out tonight, and I would hate to have that stress manifest by me shooting an innocent bystander in a case of mistaken identity. *Capice*?"

"What the hell are the Doublemint twins?" said Doug.

Porter sighed. "Out of the woods. Now," he said, pointing behind the boys. "I'd escort you myself, but I need to do a bit of a more thorough sweep first. Understand, though, that if I see you again, there will be a world of trouble. A world."

Porter sauntered back into the darkness.

"Now what?" said Trent. "I guess we've got to get out of

here, huh?"

"What are you talking about?" said Doug. "Look, you go to the Halloween dance or whatever if you want. But I'm not missing out on this. Later." He plunged into the woods in a separate direction from Porter's barely visible light.

"I think I need some new friends," Trent grumbled, then headed after Doug.

Henry hopped upwards, narrowly avoiding the fireball that presently had the ground below him sizzling and smoking, and managed to catch Vargas with a couple of punches before being blown completely backwards by a violent burst of light that glowed an ominous, inky purple. In calmer circumstances, Henry might have pondered the origins or characteristics of such an unnatural light, but at that moment, he was preoccupied by the sensation of his spine smashing up against a tree trunk. He groaned and nearly collapsed, but managed to keep his knees just steady enough to find his footing.

"Now you know how it feels to be driven into a tree," said

Vargas. "Not a pleasant sensation, is it?"

"No, 'pleasant' is *not* how I would describe it," grunted Henry, rubbing his lower back and balking at the intense tenderness. "But I'd be more than happy to help you experience it again if you'd like."

"Thank you, but that will be unnecessary. We will be finished here any moment now," said Vargas. Through eyes bleary from pain and exertion, Henry saw Vargas mumbling and gesturing once more. Somehow mustering the energy for a single explosive movement, Henry dashed in the woods, the path ahead of him briefly illuminated by a pale purple light cast by an explosion behind him that was surely cutting short the life of yet another defenseless tree. As the light faded, Henry dove behind a bush and slumped onto the ground, attempting to monitor his breathing in such a way that he could adequately refill his aching lungs while minimizing any noise that might give away his location. He had known going into this fight that it would be grueling, but his body was simply not conditioned to respond well to a war of attrition like this one. Every muscle, every joint complained in unison, and Henry was completely parched, despite having been entirely submerged in water not long before.

I'm not going to hold up this way, he thought. If I keep a frontal assault going, he's going to outlast me. My only chance to do this is do this sneakily. Guerilla-style. Maybe then…

Except there was no way that was going to work. Vargas seemed to know where Henry was at all times. He was probably moments away from popping up behind him as it was. He had been able to sense Henry *from another plane of existence*; a few square miles of forest was not likely to offer any reasonable cover at all. Vargas had said himself that Henry's aura was so potent, he could find him anywhere, anytime.

But if that was the case, how had no one, let alone Vargas, ever come for the gloves before? They had just been sitting around for who knows how long, and no attempt was ever made to obtain them that Henry was aware of. It was not as though his grandmother would have put up much of a fight if someone of Vargas's caliber had attempted to rob her of the gloves. And Henry himself was certainly no magical being without the gloves; countless embarrassments and personal failures were testament to that. So the only theory that made any logical sense was that, in order for Vargas to sense the power of the gloves, Henry had to be wearing them. Perhaps, if he removed them, Vargas would no longer be able to sense his presence. In fact, Vargas might potentially be so confused by the sudden absence of Henry's energy that he might overlook other clues to his actual whereabouts. Henry looked at the gloves on his hands intently. This was a gamble, and if Henry was wrong, Vargas would likely maim or kill him, even if it was accidental. But then, wasn't this whole situation a gamble anyway? His entire nervous system brittle and frigid, like a network of frozen wires, Henry slipped off the gloves.

Heavy footsteps plodded through the underbrush. Vargas did not bother with even the illusion of stealth at this point, and Henry was dismayed to discover that the sorcerer was even closer than he had feared. As Henry cringed, praying silently that his plan would work, the footsteps stopped. Vargas grunted, then said something in a language unlike any Henry had ever heard before, a sludgy, guttural phrase with all the tonal earmarks of a confused curse. The footsteps began to pace around, uneasily shifting directions, as Henry could hear the sounds of twigs snapping and branches being swatted aside.

"Where did you go?" Vargas called out, reverting to his version of English. "What did you do?"

It had worked. Mopping his brow, Henry plotted his next move. Running from Vargas wouldn't do him any good, as he was sure to be caught eventually. He was going to have stalk Vargas, and strike quickly, never letting Vargas get a solid fix on his position, until it was over.

Over. How exactly was this going to ever be over? Vargas clearly had no intention of giving up or striking a deal. The only way out was…no. Henry was not going to kill him. He wouldn't. He did not even believe himself capable of such a thing. But short of Vargas's death, an escape from this situation eluded him.

First thing's first, thought Henry. I've just got to beat him. We'll see where it goes from there. He crept as quietly as possible away from the bush, making a slow, wide circle around Vargas. Each step took what felt like an eternity, Henry's legs heavy with the knowledge that a single unprotected blow from Vargas in his current, vulnerable state could shatter his entire skeleton. He simply could not allow that to happen.

Henry could see the hair on the back of Vargas's head shimmering silver in the moonlight seeping through the branches above. More gray hairs seemed to sit among the dark ones than had a week before, and the hair in general was flecked and matted in places with dark spots: dirt, leaves, blood? Now was not the time for analysis. Breathing carefully, quietly, Henry slipped his gloves back on.

Vargas whirled around, eyes wide in unexpected cognizance, and was greeted with a solid right hand to the face. He hit the ground, but was up almost immediately. Despite the extreme haste of his actions, blood had already begun a steady, viscous drop from his left nostril to his chin. Individual droplets fell, perfect crimson orbs, like water from a stalactite. His pupils glowed a dim yellow with fury.

"I do not know what you are doing, or how you are doing it," Vargas said, "but it does not matter. You cannot hide from me.

You-"

A strange sensation forced Vargas to cut off his own sentence. Henry was suddenly in front of him, scythe extended, knees bent, his momentum causing his back to turn to Vargas. Vargas felt a sting across his chest, a light slash that barely broke his skin, and was cauterized nearly instantly by the implement that had delivered the wound. However, an even lighter slash across Vargas's armor materialized, meeting the previous one at nearly a ninety degree angle, and as Henry leapt away into the darkness once more, the severed corner of the armor began to sag. Bare alabaster flesh, sodden with the sweat of battle, glistened amidst the milky moonbeams. Vargas uttered loud sounds of frustration in his alien language.

Peeking out from behind a tree trunk, Henry held his gloves balled up in one sweaty fist and considered his next move. At least I have another weak spot to go after, he thought. At this rate, maybe I've got a chance.

As if reacting to Henry's thoughts, Vargas began to glow with a hellish auburn light that made it appear as though his flesh was on fire and cast the darkness of the woods into an eerie pallor.

"I will burn down this forest if you do not come forward," roared Vargas. His gravelly baritone reverberated through the trees like a tidal wave. "It means nothing to me. I will turn this entire world to ash if I must."

Henry hesitated. Vargas did not seem like to bluffing sort, and he certainly seemed capable of burning down the woods, not to mention the town beyond. St. Dante had suffered enough damage because of Vargas; Henry could not bear to be the cause of the town's ruination. To say nothing of the lives that might be lost: his friends…his family…

Henry yanked on his gloves and rushed at Vargas, thrusting an elbow at his exposed chest. Before he could connect, however, the flickering halo surrounding Vargas expanded outward, a wave of scorching force knocking Henry to the ground. As Henry scrambled to his feet, Vargas raised the hanging flap of armor to its original position and, through gritted teeth, whispered in an unintelligible rasp. Holding the flap in place, his hand glowed magma red and he gasped almost imperceptibly amidst a gooey sizzling. The glow faded, and Vargas removed his hand from his chest, to reveal an uneven raised seam where the armor had fused back together.

"I hope that was not your only plan," said Vargas.

"I can just do it again," said Henry, standing his ground. "No big deal. See, I think I've got this all figured out. You can glow bright colors and shoot fireballs and pull balloon animals out of your butt for all I care, but the fact is, *I'm* winning."

"Winning?" said Vargas. "You honestly believe that you can defeat me?"

"Well, I didn't used to," said Henry. His breathing was heavy, and he clutched his aching ribs, but grinned. "But I kinda do now."

"Whoa, whoa!" said a voice to the right of Henry, accompanied by the sound of leaves and branches whooshing in forceful chorus. Both Henry's and Vargas's heads whipped about in response to the sudden, awkward disturbance. Their eyes were met by the sight of Doug and, just behind him, Trent, half-cloaked in shadow and standing stock-still.

"What the hell, you guys?" roared Henry. "Get out of here!"

"Wow. We…um…" said Trent.

"This is…this is actually really terrifying," said Doug. "Not really that much fun."

"Yeah. Duh," said Henry, incredulous. "Beat it! You're gonna get-"

It was too late. Vargas descended upon Doug, a swift silhouette scooping up the boy by the scruff of his neck. Doug had not enough time even to squirm before he was hoisted into the air, yelping. His feet dangled in the air like low-hanging fruit; his neck muscles tensed against the five points of pressure suddenly locked around them.

"I believe this may be the end of our conflict," said Vargas. His tone held the faintest hint of glee, albeit a glee masked by noticeably labored breathing.

"You leave him alone," said Henry. "He's got nothing to do with any of this. Just put him down."

"Surely, I will," said Vargas. "Once, that is, you have agreed to accompany me back to my world on the terms we discussed previously. Otherwise…well, his life is meaningless to me. But I am certain that you cannot say the same."

"I'll kill you if you hurt him. I swear I will."

"Oh, you might. You might not. Personally, I would not suggest that we put your word to the test."

"Damn it," said Henry. "I can't believe this! Do what you want to me; that's fine. But Doug's innocent here…wouldn't letting him go be the honorable thing to do?"

"That depends on how you view honor," said Vargas, his words interlaced with the gasps and hissing profanities seeping from Doug's mouth as he writhed in mid-air. "To me, the highest form of honor is serving my people, a task to which your assistance would be a boon. Though I have no great desire to commit what you must perceive as atrocities in order to achieve this end, my sense of responsibility for my people comes above all else."

"So you're going to exploit my devotion to my friends in order to express your devotion to your people? Is that what you're saying?"

"If it is any consolation to you, I am aware of the irony,"

said Vargas. Any slight indication of pleasure or satisfaction had left his voice. All that was left was a growl. "I have the utmost respect for the fact that you care about your friends, your town, your home. I know the rage, the helplessness you must be feeling. I know it all too well. But the fact is, our desires do not align, and my needs are paramount. If I have to rip out your heart to make you my soldier, so be it."

Henry froze, unsure of his next move. He could not just give up, not after coming this far. But he certainly could not let Doug get hurt. Or worse. The noises coming from Doug were becoming increasingly hoarse and panicked, which meant that Henry had precious little time to make up his mind. A single bead of sweat trickled into his left eye, and he blinked rapidly to clear the sudden discomfort. It was the most movement he could muster at the moment.

"Shall we go?" said Vargas amidst Doug's desperate protests. "Or should I crush your friend's neck right now?"

Before Henry could even take a breath, Vargas's head pitched forward as a dull thunk reverberated through the woods. In the moonlight, Henry saw Trent clutching his flashlight like a billy club, wide-eyed and trembling after whacking Vargas in the back of the skull, paralyzed in seeming disbelief of his actions.

Vargas whipped his head toward his assailant with a maniacal snarl. Trent whimpered as he found himself under the intense gaze of the towering warrior. Henry's legs unfroze and, barely cognizant of his own actions, he bounded toward Vargas. With his left hand, he roughly shoved Doug to the ground, free from Vargas's grip, while his right hand landed a solid haymaker on Vargas's chin. Vargas spun a quarter-turn in midair and soared backwards into the darkness, an unwilling missile.

"Alright, now get the hell out of here!" Henry roared at his two shell-shocked friends.

"Yeah, I'm doing just fine, thanks," muttered Doug as he massaged his neck. It was rapidly becoming a vivid shade of purple.

"GO AWAY," Henry spat.

"He's right, Doug. Let's go," said Trent, tugging on his friend's arm in a panicked attempt to haul him away from the site before Vargas returned.

"I'm going," said Doug. He paused for a moment. "Thanks for saving my ass back there," he said, making quick eye contact with Henry. Then he and Trent fled through the trees.

Henry watched his friends' flickering flashlight beam mark their hasty retreat. A rustle jerked his attention back towards the area of the forest into which Vargas had fallen. There was nothing there but trees and darkness. Perhaps there was a raccoon or something out there, but there was certainly no trace of a hulking waxen wizard.

"Alright," said Henry in a voice that came out much quieter than he had intended. "Let's wrap this up! I ain't got all night. Where did you go?"

Silence.

"Come on. I'm right here. Isn't this what you want?"

More silence. Which somewhat paradoxically felt louder than the roar of a jet turbine.

"Damn it, come out here! Hiding in the trees is my trick…isn't it like, beneath you, or something?"

Henry was alone, or so it seemed. The leaves, shuddering in

the evening breeze, provided the only movement around him. Henry groaned, the sudden calm giving his body an unwanted chance to register its supreme soreness. Then the soreness abated in the wake of a sickening query that echoed through Henry's pounding head: what if Vargas went after Doug and Trent? He must have gone somewhere, and if wasn't observing Henry from beyond his line of sight (possible) or altogether gone in sudden retreat (quite unlikely), it certainly seemed plausible that he could be pursuing his most recent targets. If that was the case…

Henry clutched the withdrawn scythe in his tremulous right hand and clicked the button to extend it fully. Bathed in its cerulean glow, Henry surveyed the weapon's formidable blade. His worst fears about Vargas had been realized. Doug had been in very significant danger just moments ago, and if Vargas willing to harm Henry's friends in his attempts to gain Henry's service, how far would he go? Would he go after his family next? Maybe even Denise? Enraged by the thought of his loved ones being in such peril, Henry rose the blade to his face. The peculiar warmth seeping from the scythe gave him goose bumps. It was time to put an end to this whole ordeal before it became a complete tragedy. As he looked down upon the alien weapon, Henry focused upon one thought, one unavoidable realization that spread through his mind like a plague.

Vargas might just have to die.

Chapter Eleven

"Would you hurry the hell up?" huffed Trent as a pine bough smacked him right next to his eyeball.

"Jeez, sorry. Guess the almost-getting-choked-to-death thing might just be slowing me down a little," said Doug. His hand had scarcely left his neck as the boys dashed, disoriented, through the woods. "Do you even know where we're going?"

"Yes and no," said Trent. "I know where I think we should *be* going. I'm just not one hundred percent certain that we're actually headed in the right direction."

"Would you mind figuring that out, like, now?" asked Doug. "I think this flashlight's gonna go out any minute, and I'm not exactly in love with the idea of being out here in the pitch black with God-knows-what running around in these woods."

"Guess the flashlight wasn't designed to be used as a blunt-force weapon," said Trent, nearly tripping over an upraised root.

"But it's not exactly pitch black out here. We've got the moon."

"Great. Glad to hear it. So again, where are we going?"

"I was thinking," said Trent. "When this Vargas guy saw us, he knew immediately to come after us, right? He obviously knew that we were Henry's friends, not just some random passersby, right?"

"Seemed that way, yeah."

"So, then, based on that, and what Henry told us about this guy just popping up from out of nowhere, I think it's a fair assumption that Vargas has probably been keeping a pretty close eye on Henry, at least to some degree."

"Mmm-hmm. Makes sense. Vargas does seem like the type that would be prepared."

"Now assuming that Vargas has been watching Henry, and that he recognized us as his friends and decided to threaten us-"

"It was more threatening *me* than *us*. And more choking than threatening," Doug interjected. He accidentally caught a leaf in his open mouth and spat it out with confused agitation.

"Either way," said Trent, "he might come after us again. By

extension, if he's aiming to get at the people he recognizes as Henry's friends, who he knows Henry to hang around with regularly…then who else might he have in his crosshairs?"

"Aw, crap," groaned Doug. "Albert. He has no idea."

"My thoughts exactly," said Trent. "So I think we ought to swing by the high school and warn him. I don't know exactly how much we can even do to defend ourselves, but it's better than nothing."

"Agreed. We'd better get over there. It beats cowering at home, I guess. Although I'm beginning to see that appeal of that," said Doug. "Now can we please hurry the hell up before the light goes out?"

"The moon, man. We've got the moon," said Trent. His voice was little more than a gasp as he pointed up to the shrouded sky.

"Oh, shut up," said Doug, who somehow managed to catch another stray leaf in his mouth before spitting it out in a spiteful spray of saliva.

Sheriff Porter exhaled through pursed lips as he surveyed the two well-dressed men currently captured in the gallingly bright beam of his flashlight. "You all right there, fellas?" he asked rhetorically.

"Mfffrgrrrbrr," Tyker managed to say.

"We've been better," sighed Foley. "My shoulder's blasted to hell, and my partner here quite clearly has at the very least, a badly shattered jaw, judging by his current vocabulary."

"That explains it," said Porter, squinting at the two agents. "I was thinking maybe he was one of those mentally special types."

"Well, I guess you could argue that regardless," mused Foley.

"Grrfllbbrr," growled Tyker.

"So you can imagine that I'm quite curious about a couple things," said Porter lazily. "One, what are two such dapper gentlemen doing out in the middle of the woods on Halloween night? And two, what on God's green earth happened to the two of you that made you such a couple of wrecks?" He tilted his head and looked Foley up and down. "Judging by your friend's predicament,

I suppose you'll have to be the one to provide me the answers, if you will."

"Of course," said Foley. "I'd be more than happy to. You see-"

A thunderous metallic crash ended Foley's sentence prematurely, as all three men twisted their necks to face the source of the noise. Something had collided with Porter's police car. Something with a tremendous amount of force behind it.

"Aw, damn it," Henry groaned as he rubbed his forehead and surveyed the damage. "One thing after another."

"And just what the hell do you think you're doing?" Porter bellowed, his hand instinctively reaching for the pistol at his waist.

"Oh God, yeah, sorry," Henry said. "Really. I'm sorry. I'm in a huge hurry and I wasn't looking where I was going and…yikes. I am *so* sorry."

"Sorry?" said Porter. "You wrecked my car, you little idiot! Do you have any idea what the penalty for vandalizing an officer's vehicle is?"

"Look, seriously, I apologize," Henry stammered. "But I

don't have time for this right now."

"You'd better make time, then, you-"

"Sorry!" called Henry as he bounded through the forest, whooshing past the three men like a miniature hurricane. The police car creaked, bemoaning its ruined frame.

"This is unbelievable!" groaned Porter, beside himself. "He just takes off, just like that! Who in the hell does he think he is? Who does he expect to pay for this?"

"Don't look at me," shrugged Foley. "Ow. Shouldn't shrug."

"Ssfrgrll," said Tyker.

Albert was attempting to contain his profuse sweat by sheer force of will. He was also in the process of figuring out exactly what to do with himself as Jenny wrapped her arms around him and gyrated. Clad in the hat, mustache and red overalls of the more famous half of video game duo the Super Mario Bros. (a last minute Halloween costume decision after weeks of dwelling on the topic), he felt lumbering and goofy compared to Jenny in her sleek little devil girl outfit. At least the color schemes matched. Albert had never been in a situation like this before, and he typically loathed the awkwardness of being unsure of which course of action to take in any given situation. In this particular case, though, he did not mind at all. But his glee was accompanied by an unfortunate amount of anxious moisture. Maybe if he just focused hard enough, he could rein it in…

"Loosen up," said Jenny, beaming up at Albert as she danced. "You don't have to be nervous."

"I'm…oh, I'm loose," said Albert hurriedly. He hoped he was managing to avoid blushing. "I'm not nervous at all. I'm, um, I'm having a great time."

"Good. Me too," said Jenny. She continued to dance as Albert attempted a few shaky steps.

The serenity of the moment was shattered by an exclamation that, though raspy, was unmistakably Doug's. "Oh, there we go. Albert! Yo, Albert!"

"Excuse me just a second," Albert murmured, apologetic, as he turned from Jenny in the direction of the voice.

"Dude, I'm glad we found you! Nice 'stache," said Doug, clasping his hand on Albert's shoulder. He then glanced over at Albert's date, who was smiling faintly. "Oh. Hi Jenny."

"Hi," she said with a wave.

"Hi," said Trent, popping up behind Doug.

"Oh, hi," said Albert.

"OK, if all the hi-ing is finished now, we need to talk to you about something," said Doug, motioning for Albert to follow him.

"What's going on?" said Albert, looking ruefully at Jenny over his shoulder as he shuffled away.

"Henry's fighting Vargas right now. At this moment in time," said Trent. "And so far he's looking pretty good. He hasn't lost, anyway."

"Well hey, that's great!" said Albert. "But how would you know? I thought Henry told you guys to stay away from-"

"Look, regardless of what we were told, we, uh, happened upon the fight, and we watched some of it. And Henry was definitely holding his own. But there's a problem."

"Oh, no. What?" Albert gulped.

"Henry might have been putting up a little too good of a fight. Vargas saw us watching, grabbed me and held me hostage. Just about killed me," said Doug, absent-mindedly rubbing his throat.

"But Henry saved you," said Albert.

"Henry and *I* saved him," said Trent. He glared at Doug. "Which I don't think I ever got thanked for."

"I did thank you!" said Doug, rolling his eyes. "I specifically said, 'Thank you.' What else do you want, a fruit basket?"

"You said 'thank you' to Henry, not to me."

"It was a blanket statement! A blanket thank you!"

"OK, anyway…" said Albert, looking back at Jenny.

"Yeah, anyway, so we got away from that whole situation, but we wanted to warn you about Vargas," said Doug. "He attacked me, and he seemed to be aware that we were Henry's friends, not just two random guys in the woods. And if he knows that about us, he probably knows it about you too, since we figure he must have been keeping an eye on Henry for a while."

"So be careful," said Trent. "Just be on the lookout for

him."

"And if he finds me? What am I supposed to do?" said Albert. "And furthermore, aren't you guys a little bit worried that he followed you back here? I mean, I appreciate the heads-up, but what if you just led him here, right to me and the whole rest of the school?"

"Um," said Doug, "I suppose that would be a bad thing. But try not to worry about it too much…Henry seemed to be keeping him pretty busy."

"Yeah, and even if he kidnaps Henry or kills him or something, I don't think Vargas would have much reason to come here. He'd be done, he could go home," said Trent. As both Doug and Albert glared at him, clucking with disgust at the callous comment, Trent shrugged. "What?"

Albert started to respond, but before he could utter much more than a syllable, his words caught in his throat and his complexion gained a striking whiteness. As Doug and Trent turned their heads to partake in whatever vision had caused Albert's sudden transformation, their stomachs churned in anticipation of what they already knew they were going to see.

Vargas stood towering in the entrance of the high school gymnasium, his pale flesh cast into an eerie shade of orange by the string of jack-o-lantern-shaped LED lights that hung about the doorway. He was scanning the crowd for something; Doug, Trent and Albert could only assume that the something in question was them.

"I really hate being wrong," groaned Doug.

"We've gotta get out of here," said Trent.

"What about Jenny?" said Albert. "I can't just leave her here!"

"Trust me, she'll be better off if we're far away from her," said Doug. "I don't think she's on Vargas's radar yet. We should probably keep it that way."

"Then how are we going to get out of here?" said Albert, ducking to avoid Vargas's line of sight. "He's standing in the doorway. I don't think we can get past him without being noticed."

"There's gotta be an emergency exit somewhere, right? The fire code must require something like that," said Trent.

"Do you really want to be running around looking for an exit while he's looking for us?" said Albert.

"No, not really," said Trent.

"Let's just hide," said Doug. "Let's find a place to hide where we can keep an eye on him. Once he leaves the doorway, we can sneak out. Piece of cake."

"Piece of cake," Albert lamented.

"Hey, at least you have a disguise," said Doug.

"Over here," said Trent. "Come on."

The three boys crept, hunched over, through the crowd, toward a tall speaker surrounded by various audio equipment in the corner of the room. They did not even notice the quizzical looks from some of their classmates as the squatting conga line passed them by. When they reached the corner, they scrambled for cover behind the equipment and peeked over at Vargas, who appeared to be talking to one of the chaperones.

"Excuse me, sir," said the chaperone. "This is a school function, for students and chaperones only. If you're not a chaperone, I'm going to have to ask you to leave."

Vargas casually punched the chaperone in the face. A tooth flew out of the chaperone's mouth as his consciousness flicked off in an instant. As he hit the ground, another, larger man rushed over to Vargas.

"Look, buddy," said the chaperone, "I don't know what the hell you think you're doing, but I'm calling the-"

Another brutal punch left another prone body on the floor. Vargas closed the gym door behind him and dug into a small pouch on the back of his suit, producing a length of some sort of rope or cable. The students began taking notice of the commotion and an uneasy chatter arose on the dance floor as Vargas wound the cable around the door handles and tied it off, then pushed on the door handles to make sure they were securely bound shut. Satisfied at his work, he whisked through the crowd, which parted in terror of his imposing figure, and headed to the DJ booth on the stage. No one, student or chaperone, dared try to halt him or even speak to him. The DJ himself, a spiky-haired fellow from the local hip-hop radio station, wilted as he became engulfed in Vargas's shadow.

"Is this the microphone?" Vargas asked, pointing at the

mike in the DJ's quivering hand. "Will this project my voice throughout the auditorium?"

The DJ nodded, though his shakes would have approximated a nod even if his response had been negative. Vargas grabbed the microphone, which the DJ relinquished all too readily, and turned his attention to the crowd. He began to speak, but even his booming voice was muffled by the loud music blaring through the speakers.

"Turn this damned music off," Vargas said tersely, eyeing the DJ, who may have set a new world record for fastest response time to a command. As the music abruptly terminated, the anxious murmur of the crowd became audible, draping the room in a dense fog of dread.

"Good evening," said Vargas. "Do not worry, I have no intention of taking up any more of your time than I must. I wish I did not have to be here at all. But, alas, here I am, and for that you can thank a compatriot of yours, one Henry Garrison. You no doubt know of whom I speak, do you not?" Several heads throughout the auditorium nodded, several shook, and the majority just stared ahead, dumbfounded. "Excellent, I see that many of you do," Vargas continued. "Then we can make this quick, and I will be on my way. I want one of you to tell me, right now, if Henry Garrison is in this building somewhere. For your sake, I hope that he is. Because if he is not, I am afraid I am going to have to use you all to get him here, through means that may prove…unsavory." As Vargas said this, he put down the microphone and began an incantation. His hands glowed an unnatural shade of vermillion, and the speaker to his right erupted in a column of flame, scattering sparks, wires and bits of circuitry into the crowd. The multitude's murmur of anxiety erupted into a full on panic, as the students shrieked and stampeded, and a few brave souls tried unsuccessfully to break down the gymnasium door.

Vargas picked up the microphone again and, the smoldering speaker casting a devilish light on his face, said, "Stop. Be silent." When his command went largely unheeded, he repeated in a roar like the ocean at highest tide, "STOP. BE SILENT."

The students became quiet, albeit fidgety. From amid the mass, a voice yelled out, "Here's not here! We don't know where he is!"

"How unfortunate," said Vargas. He looked down at the floor before refocusing on the audience. "Then I am afraid things are going to get a bit messy for you."

"Oh God," Albert whispered.

"Shut up," Trent whispered.

"Where the hell is Henry?" Doug whispered. "This is no good."

"Duh," Albert said.

"Shut *up*," Trent hissed.

A boom like a thunderclap shook the room. The students near the doors backed off as a second boom rattled the door frame.

"Ah," mused Vargas, dropping the microphone. "Here we are."

A third blow caved in the doors in significantly, and a fourth sent them crashing to the floor with an authoritative slam. As the sound reverberated through the ears of each terrified would-be dancer, Henry Garrison strode into the room.

"Vargas!" he barked. "This has nothing to do with them.

Leave 'em alone and let's just finish things between us."

"Oh, we will finish things," said Vargas, "but I see no reason to do so on your terms. Do as I say, or the lives of all of your peers will be forfeit. Starting with one of your dear friends."

Before Henry could so much as utter a response, Vargas had plunged into the crowd and zeroed in on Roderick King III and Denise Hargrove, masquerading as a pair of vampires. Denise wept and buried her face in Roderick's shoulder as the wizard reached out his hand to them.

The force of Vargas's grip caused Roderick to stagger back a step, and Denise ducked under Vargas's arm and ran into the crowd, bawling. Roderick wheezed and kicked, his cape fluttering as the wizard effortlessly lifted him off the ground by his throat.

"Son of a-" Roderick gasped. "You don't know-"

"What do you say now, Garrison?" said Vargas, a syrupy tone of triumph oozing over his words. "I will not make the same mistake twice. I will snap the boy's neck at a moment's notice if you do not agree to accompany me right this instant."

Henry surveyed the scene with a quizzical look. He stared at

Roderick squirming in Vargas grasp and raised an eyebrow. Then, despite his best efforts to compose himself, he started to giggle. With moments, the giggle built into a full-fledged peal of laughter.

"Have you lost your mind?" snarled Vargas.

Unable to contain his laughter, Henry bellowed, "You idiot! I guess your ability to read situations isn't quite what you thought it was, huh? Do whatever you want to him, I don't care. While you waste your time with him, I'll demolish you. I'm sure he'd be more than happy to make the sacrifice for my sake. Now wouldn't you, Rod?"

"The hell-" Roderick wheezed.

"What are you talking about?" said Vargas. "I have seen you speak to this boy on numerous occasions. You two seems like brothers, roughhousing."

"Yeah. Brothers. That's exactly how I would describe it," Henry said, sneering. He extended the scythe in his right hand. "So why don't you make us *blood* brothers? Go ahead."

"You crazy…freak…" Roderick said. His struggles were getting weaker, more desperate.

"You must be bluffing," said Vargas, tightening his grip as Roderick squawked.

"Try me," said Henry. "Be my guest."

"No…don't…" said Roderick, barely audibly.

"You know what, though?" said Henry, squinting at Roderick's increasingly ineffectual thrashing. "I kind of feel bad for him, so how about this: I'll give you my scythe here, and you let him go. Does that work for you?"

"So you do care," said Vargas.

"Not really," said Henry. "And certainly not enough to give in to you. But this is kind of pitiful, and besides, maybe if you've got a weapon, you might have some chance of actually beating me."

"Is that correct?" said Vargas. "Your hubris is appalling, but fine. As you wish. Throw it over here, and we can finally end this farce."

Henry stared at the scythe in his hand and exhaled. He shifted it from his right hand to his left and balled up his free fist. If this was going to work, there was no room for error. With a silent prayer, he tossed the weapon to Vargas, who snatched it in midair with a cruel grin. A gruesome sizzling sound emanated from Vargas's palm as his grin turned into a scream. He swiftly dropped both Roderick and the scythe and instinctively clutched at his wounded hand. By the time Roderick hit the floor, Henry was on the move, and threw a punch straight at Vargas's skull with all the speed he could muster.

Vargas grabbed Henry by the wrist a fraction of a second before the punch could connect. "Nice try," he said, wincing as his singed skin clutched rough leather.

Henry squatted and grabbed the scythe in his free hand, then slashed at Vargas with wild abandon. Vargas's eyes widened and he lunged backwards, but the tip of the blade tore across his chest despite his retreat. Pressing his advantage, Henry reached his left hand out and grabbed hold of the fresh tear across Vargas's suit. The scythe resting against Henry's palm seared Vargas's bare skin as Henry yanked the wizard toward him and delivered a solid uppercut to Vargas's jaw. Vargas's eyes rolled around in his skull and he dropped to one knee. Before Henry could gloat, Vargas sunk his fist into Henry's gut, and the boy collapsed to his knees with an agonized groan. The two combatants squinted at each other, finally eye-to-eye.

The atmosphere within the gymnasium was rapidly changing. More than half of the students and faculty had fled once the entrance was clear, but a circle of several dozen people surrounded Henry and Vargas, enthralled by the rare event taking place before them. Doug, Trent and Albert remained hidden in the corner, but peeked out and paid very close attention to the ongoing battle. The DJ slumped down in his chair, his heart still pounding, piston-like, from his encounter with Vargas. As he looked out over the room, he became increasingly confused about exactly what was going on. Was this some sort of elaborate prank? Was this just a high school full of weirdoes with a flair for the dramatic? He decided that, regardless of the nature of the events unfolding before him, he was pretty interested in what might happen next. And besides, he *had* been paid for the full duration of the evening. May as well do his job.

As Henry stared at Vargas, wondering just how much more the wizard had left in the tank, he shuddered at the sudden jarring blaring of music through the remaining undamaged speakers. His initial shock was in no way soothed by the realization of just what sort of music it was.

Everybody was kung fu fightiiiiiiing…

"You've gotta be freaking kidding me," said Henry under his shallow breath.

The split-second distraction was enough for Vargas to make his move. Shaky but swift, he tackled Henry. In turn, Henry's reflexes kicked in and as he tumbled backwards, he was as surprised as anyone to find that the pointed tip of his scythe had pierced Vargas's left shoulder. The forward momentum of Vargas's attack had caused him to be deeply impaled on the end of the weapon, and as the spear continued to burn within him, his shoulders shuddered and his forehead seeped sweat.

Holding the scythe tightly, Henry leaned in and said, "Give up. That's enough. That's enough."

Vargas looked Henry right in the eye and, in a tremulous bass, said, "No. I am not finished."

"Just stop," Henry said in a voice barely above a whisper.

Sheer frustration was causing his eyes to mist up.

"Not until I have what I want," said Vargas. He began to mumble strange words, and his hands glowed like sinister jack-o-lanterns.

Henry was overcome by a flood of disturbing mental imagery…he saw his classmates shrieking as they burned alive…his friends being tortured until he finally relented to Vargas's demands…and like that, he lost control.

"No!" he roared at Vargas, and rushed toward him with uncanny speed, head butting him as the spear dug even deeper into the wizard. The light around Vargas's curled fingers was snuffed, and the wizard began to slump as Henry punched him solidly in the side of the head once, then again. A third punch knocked Vargas backwards, and his head hit the varnished floor with a sickening thump.

Henry staggered to his feet, slowly regaining his composure as the crowd surveyed him with gape-mouthed awe. He withdrew the scythe's tip from Vargas's shoulder, any stray blood instantly vaporized by the blade's immense, unearthly heat. His head was pounding, and he figured that his body's adrenaline reserves had to be running pretty dry. Every breath he took, no matter how shallow, was accompanied by a sharp pain that indicated something broken inside him. But at least he was still standing.

Henry's dreamy self-examination was disrupted by a glimpse of Vargas's mouth moving. The wizard's gaze met Henry's through swollen eyelids, and his mouth curled into a hateful sneer. Tremors rippled across the floor as Henry knelt down and grabbed Vargas by the tear in his suit. His muscles screaming for rest, Henry lifted Vargas up with one hand. Even as Henry lifted him as high as possible, Vargas's feet barely seemed to be off the ground. As Vargas's chanting continued, the rumbling grew more intense, and several students panicked and tumbled over. Vargas reached out and grasped Henry's upper arms in his hands, and despite his relatively feeble strength, his grip was steely. Henry ended the chanting abruptly as he raked the back of his fist against Vargas's face. Finally the enormous man fell limp. With a grunt, Henry heaved him over his shoulder. Vargas's fingers dragged on the ground and Henry made a few labored steps.

"That one was for destroying my lunch box," he muttered.

Doug, Albert and Trent rushed up as the rest of the room chattered and squealed about the incredible events they had just witnessed. "Are you OK, man?" said Doug.

"Yeah. Barely," said Henry. He held his sore side with his free hand. "Doubt I'll be doing any gymnastics anytime soon."

"Like your lazy ass would ever do any gymnastics anyway," snorted Doug.

Henry laughed, then tightened his grip on his side as pain radiated through his chest.

"Is he dead?" said Albert, motioning at Vargas. "He looks-"

"Nah," said Henry, "I can feel him breathing. A little bit. Unless that's just my tremors, but I can't really take the chance. I've gotta go deal with him before he wakes up."

"What're you-" said Trent.

"Later. I'll explain it later," said Henry. He headed toward the doorway, then turned his head back. "I'm really glad you guys are all safe."

Before Henry could reach the doorway, Denise stepped out

in front of him. "Wait a second," she said.

Henry blinked and sucked on his teeth. "Hey, I'm sorry," he said. "I hope you understand now why I couldn't commit to going to the dance with you. I had, well, *this* to deal with."

"So you knew this was coming?" she said.

"Sort of," he said. "I knew I was gonna have to fight this guy." He patted Vargas's slumped body. "I didn't know it was gonna spill over into here, and I didn't know that I was going to win. That's just kind of the way it turned out."

"I understand. Actually, maybe I don't understand. But I get what you're saying," she said. She looked at the floor. "Were you really willing to just let Roderick die back there? I mean, I know you saved him, but to be honest, you didn't seem like you would have cared if you hadn't."

"I had to think on my feet there, so I guess I was bluffing. I didn't mean it, mostly. It was the Br'er Rabbit Briar Patch strategy. Reverse psychology."

"And if it didn't work?"

"I didn't really think that far ahead," said Henry sheepishly.

"Can we talk about this some other time?"

"Sure," said Denise. She stared at him. "I'm not sure whether I should slap you or kiss you."

"Take your time to figure it out," Henry said. "I don't really have the energy to deal with either right now. Happy Halloween, Denise." And with that, he trudged out the door. Despite the general level of excitement coursing through the gym, everyone was too afraid of the massive bulk Henry was carrying around to make any attempt to detain him. Unwavering, he vanished into the night.

"Well, that was completely insane," said Doug. "I'm still not sure someone didn't slip LSD into my Halloween candy."

"I gotta go check on Jenny," said Albert, and he dashed off in search of his erstwhile date.

"Do you really think that's it?" said Trent. "What do you think Henry's gonna do with that guy?"

"I don't know," said Doug. "But honestly, I've had enough of this for one night. Henry's handled things well so far, and I'm sure he'll finish things up just fine. At this point, I don't even want to think about it."

"Do you think Henry'll kill him?" said Trent.

"What did I just say?" snapped Doug.

Sheriff Porter rushed into the gymnasium with the most swiftness he had mustered in the better part of two decades. Whipping his head around, he viewed the still-burning speaker on the stage, the chipped and cracked floor, and the myriad Halloween decorations strewn about.

"Is everyone OK?" he asked. He walked up to Roderick, who was rubbing his throat gingerly. "What the hell happened here?"

"What happened?" said Roderick. "Henry Garrison happened, that's what."

Vargas opened his eyes and was immediately overcome by a plethora of incredibly unpleasant sensations. His entire body had reached levels of aching he would have previously though impossible, and his shoulder in particular suffered from a sharp pain that seemed to burrow down into his very soul. His reluctant attempts to move were thwarted by a binding of great tensile strength, and he wriggled sideways on the ground like a recently hooked fish.

"Good, you're awake," said a voice, causing Vargas's head to jerk up to look at the source and suffer the consequential soreness in his neck. Henry stood over Vargas, backlit by the massive yellow moon. From what Vargas could gather, they were in some sort of alley, and quite alone.

"This rope or whatever that you had on you is something else. I've never seen anything like it," said Henry as a twirled a length of the cord Vargas had used to bind the gymnasium doors shut between his fists. "I don't even know if it's breakable at all, but it's so thin! I'll say this, your people must have some crazy science."

"What is the point of this?" said Vargas. "You are clearly not going to kill me, or you would have done so already. You are just wasting my time and yours with this nonsense."

"Am I?" said Henry. He turned to look up at the moon. "Maybe you're right. Maybe this is a waste of time. But it's a waste of *your* time, not mine. I'm not the one who's completely helpless right now, far from home. I'm exactly where I want to be, free to do whatever I want. And you, well, you're completely at my mercy right now. So let me ask you a question: how badly do you want to help your people?"

"That is an asinine question. All of my efforts have been for my people. You know how far I would go."

"I do, I do. At least to some extent. I doubt I've seen the limits of just how far you'd be willing to go, nor do I want to see them. But I have to wonder just how much good you're doing your people by being here, tied up and useless. Bear in mind, I don't exactly have any motivation to let you go. And I highly doubt you'll be freeing yourself anytime soon, especially with the shape you're in."

Vargas lay there silent, his face a twisted mask of contempt.

"So here's what I'm suggesting to you," said Henry, twirling the retracted scythe between his fingertips. "You go home, and you do what you've got to do there, and you leave me alone. You're already in rough shape, and even though I'm not going to kill you, I have no problem *keeping* you in rough shape, or putting you in even rougher shape, if it keeps me and my friends safe. You've done quite enough around here, and I won't have you threatening anyone ever again."

"I have come to see that we are not so dissimilar, you and I," said Vargas, adjusting himself a bit to lay flat on his back and stare up into the stars. "We are both willing to go to extraordinary lengths to protect those we care about. Although I would say that you are likely more motivated by self-preservation than I am, I suppose I made that necessary by my actions. But you would never allow your friends come to harm, if you can prevent it."

"Of course not," said Henry. "So please don't make it necessary for me to have to protect them from you anymore."

Vargas sighed, then groaned at the pain his sigh caused. "Fine. This is very embarrassing, but I will not trouble you any longer. You have earned that courtesy. But I will do so only on one condition."

"And what might that be?"

"I want your weapon. Your scythe. Give it to me, and I will leave you in peace."

"You've got some nerve, dude," Henry fumed. "After all

this, you're completely at a disadvantage, helpless, and yet you have the gall to try and make some kind of trade with me? Besides which, do you really think I'm so stupid that I'll let you go *and* give you my ridiculously cool weapon so you can just turn around and tear me up with it? You must have taken a few too many blows to the head."

"I understand how it sounds," said Vargas. "And I am certain that taking me at my word cannot be easy for you. But despite my actions, you cannot say that I have ever lied to you or misled you in any way. My word is good, and always has been. However, I am not returning home without something to show for my efforts, and your scythe would aid me greatly in my quest."

"You'll have to excuse me for not being overly worried about your pride and well-being at the moment," said Henry.

"You are excused," said Vargas. "But these are the terms of my deal. Give me the scythe, and I will no longer bother you."

"Well, if we're going to be making demands here, I'll need some sort of insurance policy that you're not just going to take it, go heal up, and then come right back after me again. How can you prove to me that I'll be safe after I contribute to making you more dangerous?"

"I cannot prove it to you in any way other than giving you my word," said Vargas. "But I assure you, if you try to keep me captive here, I will eventually free myself, and when I do, I would be far more dangerous than I will be if you let me go right now. After this experience, I have no desire to fight you again, but if I am to be your prisoner, then you can be certain that I will exact vengeance upon you, sooner or later."

"I don't think you're really in a position to threaten me right now," said Henry, kneeling next to Vargas. "So you'd better watch it."

"Simply accept my offer, and this will be over with," said Vargas. "My people need me; I have no desire to dally around here any longer."

Henry clicked the button on the cylinder and extended the scythe, illuminating Vargas in a shade of ghastly blue. "Fine, but no funny business," he said as he lowered the blade toward Vargas's bindings. "And I guess it's not like you can use this thing against me anyways. You remember what it did to your hand when you tried to hold it."

"Vividly."

"Then take it, and go. Tell you the truth, I don't want the damn thing anyway. Always gave me the creeps," said Henry as he cut through the cord. "But I swear to God, if you break the terms of this deal…"

"Absolutely not. You need not worry about that," said Vargas. He pushed himself to his knees with great difficulty, then picked up a mossy green stone from the ground beside him.

"Hey now, what the hell do you think you're doing?" said Henry, pointing the tip of the scythe at Vargas's face.

"I wish to give you something," said Vargas. "I feel it is important that you have this." He rubbed the stone between his fingers and muttered some of his strange gibberish. The stone began to emit a soft emerald glow.

"Stop it!" said Henry. "I'm not gonna let you-"

Vargas's mumbling stopped. "Do not worry," he said. "This will not harm you. I merely enchanted this so that you have a means of communicating me. It is less than ideal, but lacking anything more suitable, it must suffice. If you should ever change your mind and decide that you might wish to aid me, just crack this stone, which should be no issue for someone of your strength, and I shall appear before you." He pressed the stone into Henry's hand as he finally got to his feet.

'And why on earth would I ever, in a million years, want to do that?" Henry said, rolling his eyes.

"Various reasons," said Vargas. "You never know. You may need my help some day. Then perhaps we can work out a deal where you could lend me your services as well."

"Let me tell you something," said Henry dryly. He retracted the scythe and handed it to Vargas, who tapped it to make sure it was harmless before he hesitantly grabbed it. "The only way I can conceive of ever needing your help again is if you decide to unleash another huge monster on the city."

Vargas laughed, a hearty guffaw with a side of cough. "Wouldn't dream of it. Farewell," he said. He lowered his head and began to chant. A milky yellow circle materialized around him as his chanting grew fiercer. A wailing wind whooshed through the alley as Henry staggered backwards. The yellow light enveloped Vargas's body as the howling wind grew stronger, like the shrieks of banshees. Then, like that, Vargas was gone, and all was still.

Henry stood dumbfounded, swaying on his feet. "I'll be damned," he said. "The bastard actually used a contraction." At this, his body gave out, and he slumped over in the alleyway and slipped into oblivion's comforting embrace.

From behind a dumpster a few dozen feet away, Roderick King III curiously surveyed Henry's crumpled form with a sly smirk.

Chapter Twelve

Henry's time in the hospital was mercifully brief. His doctor was awed by the brutal extent of his injuries when he was first brought in, and just as awed at how quickly Henry's body healed from his wounds. Within a couple days, Henry was cleared to go home, his fractured ribs tightly wrapped, with a stern warning to take it easy for the time being, lest he risk aggravating his injuries. Henry was only too happy to oblige.

Upon his release, Henry headed for the sheriff's office. As he entered the building, he saw Sheriff Porter sitting at his desk, sipping a cup of what one would assume to be coffee. The Sheriff was shaking his head and he rifled through a stack of paperwork, mouthing the words as he read them.

"Hi, uh, excuse me? Sheriff?" said Henry.

"Oh no," said Porter as he raised his head in a sloth-like manner. "The resident celebrity. Well, I appreciate you saving me the trouble of having to come drag you out of the hospital, I guess."

"Yeah, thanks," said Henry. "Listen, I-"

"You what?" said Porter. "You wrecked another car? Smashed up another building? I swear to you, Garrison, if I had a cell that I thought would hold you I would put you under lock and key right now. You have no idea what I've been through the past few weeks due to you and you alone."

"That's why I'm here," said Henry. "I'm sorry for all the trouble I've caused. I never intended on being involved in anything like this."

"Your intentions mean exactly jack diddly to me, Garrison," said Porter. "I've been wracking my brain to figure out just how many charges I should bring you up on, but I'm not sure my old noggin is capable of processing numbers that big. I'll say this: I have never seen a public menace like you before in my life, and I've seen some real hooligans, let me tell you."

"I apologize. Truly," said Henry, scratching the back of his neck. "And I wanted to make you an offer. It's not much, but it's the least I can do, given all that's happened."

"If you're going to buy me a new patrol car, well, then that's a start."

"Um, no. I don't have the money to be buying, well, anything, really. But I have something that I think is more valuable than money. I want to offer you my services as, I don't know, a deputy or something? Is that how it works?"

"How it works?" said Porter. "Are you seriously coming to me with this nonsense?"

"Well, uh, yes. Yes I am. I mean, think about it: I know I have a huge debt to this town to work off. So let me work for you. Let me make this right. You could have a super-strong, incredibly durable, fast and efficient police officer. Or deputy, or, you know, whatever. There would be no such thing as a crisis in this town, because I could take care of anything that comes up. You could relax, knowing that no matter what happens, we're equipped to deal with it. That sounds pretty good, right?"

Porter stood up from behind his desk and leveled a heavy scowl in Henry's direction. "No, Garrison, it does not sound 'pretty good.' And as far as a crisis in this town, I can't recall any occurring before you brought out your little magic act and started ripping the place to shreds."

"What? But I think-"

"Listen. I don't care what you think. Let me make this very clear for you: I don't want you on my force. Now, or ever. All I know is this: there have been exactly two catastrophes lately, and you've been involved in both of them. Now it seems you helped this town out in each case, and I suppose I should thank you for that, even if the battered vehicle in my driveway makes that exceptionally difficult. But the fact is, this kind of…excitement seems to attach itself to you. I don't like excitement. Excitement comes with destruction and a body count. You know what else was exciting, Garrison? Vietnam was exciting. I don't need that here. And so no, I'm afraid I can't use you for anything. In fact, if I had the ability to do so, I would exile you from St. Dante and never have to concern myself with seeing your face again. I know that, deep down, you're not a bad kid. I get that. But if you're going to hang around here, the best advice I can give you is to stay out of trouble. Period. I don't want us to end up on opposing sides, and we're already very, very close to that."

"Oh, believe me," said Henry with a nervous chortle, "I have every intention of staying of out trouble. But I really could be a huge asset to you, and if you could just see-"

"Go home, Garrison," said Porter, sitting back down. "You're hurt. I appreciate what you're trying to do, but the answer is no. The biggest help you can provide me is not putting yourself in another situation where I have to talk to you."

"But-"

"Go home, I said. When you're feeling better, I'm going to need a full report of everything that happened on Halloween. I got plenty of accounts, but I have a lot of questions for you. So rest up, because it's going to be a marathon next time I see you."

Henry excited the building and was immediately wrapped in a blanket of chilly November air. He looked down the street at people raking leaves, sweeping their porches and discarding their quickly moldering jack-o-lanterns. As he stuffed his hands in his pockets, he felt a rough cardboard edge against his fingertips. He pulled out an extraordinarily plain business card.

"James Foley."

With his free hand, Henry pulled out his cell phone and began to dial each digit of the phone number deliberately. A chill ran down his spine as put the phone up to his ear.

"I'm glad you called," James Foley said as he sat on the corner of his desk. Henry was seated in a leather chair facing Foley, leaning in with his elbows on his knees despite his attempts to relax. Foley tapped the sling on his arm. "It's quite a relief that getting this wasn't a wasted effort."

Tom Tyker leaned up against the wall. He jaw was wired, and it made his breathing wet and heavy. "I don't know, Jim," he wheezed through gritted teeth. His words were billowy and slurred. "Having my jaw shattered and getting interrogated by some damn hick cop were the absolute highlights of my month so far."

"You know, you could always just try not talking at all," said Foley. Tyker grunted and growled something unintelligible whose tone indicated obscenity.

"So how does this work exactly?" said Henry. "I've never

had so much as a paper route, let alone…whatever this is."

"It's pretty simple," said Foley. "You'll get a certain salary. What we need in exchange is your willingness to help us out in crises of an unusual nature. We won't bring you in for anything pedestrian unless we have no other option, as we feel it's best to limit your visibility, for your sake and ours. But from time to time, things happen, like-"

"Like when that huge monster thing attacked St. Dante," said Henry.

"Exactly. You may not believe it, but every once in a while disturbances of that nature occur. Dealing with them has traditionally been extraordinarily difficult, made even more so by the need to keep such matters as confidential as possible to prevent widespread panic. We've only gotten along so far due to a generous helping of luck, and with you in our corner, we'll have to be much less reliant on that."

"I see. Doesn't sound too bad."

"Don't get me wrong," said Foley. "You *will* be in danger in these situations. We'll back you up with what we have, but that is by no means a guarantee of success. A lot depends on you and your ability to handle these things. I don't mean to scare you, but it's only fair that I warn you: there is the very real possibility of death if things go bad."

"I understand," said Henry, leaning back, "but after what I've been through, I'm pretty confident in my abilities. Plus, these things don't come up very often, as you said, and I doubt you'd have reached out to me if you thought I couldn't handle this."

"Exactly. You're right." said Foley. "You'll rarely be called upon, if history is any indication. I mean, it's not like you're getting paid for nothing, and if we need you, you'd better damn well be there post haste. But realistically, based on what we've seen thus far, I don't think this is going to be much of a problem for you."

"Me either. If all I have to do in exchange for my paycheck is be part of some occasional excitement, that sounds good to me. It's not like you see guys of Vargas's caliber come in and wreck shop very often, right?"

"No, certainly not," said Foley. "That was a first for me, dealing with something on that level. It still blows my mind that you took him down."

"Vargas," spat Tyker. "I swear if I ever see that rotten bastard again, I'll have his ass on a platter."

"Yeah, well. No biggie. Anyway," said Henry, "sounds like a plan. Let's do this."

"There is one other thing," said Foley, rising from his desk. "Due to your…unique nature, there is a matter of concern surrounding you. As I told you before, certain people are less than thrilled at the idea of a person capable of immense destruction being able to walk around unfettered. So part of our deal is that we're going to be keeping a close eye on you. Nothing too invasive, understand; we just need to make sure that you remain on the side of the angels, as it were."

"Hmm," said Henry, cocking an eyebrow. "That's not exactly in line with what you told me before, you know. Something about not having enough funding…?"

"Ah," said Foley. "The situation is a bit different now, especially once you actively expressed an interest in our program. We've gotten a sudden and quite drastic increase in funding.

Otherwise, we'd barely have been able to pay your salary, let alone anything else. Sorry if it seems I've misled you."

"I understand," said Henry. "I was probably going to be watched anyway, so I appreciate you being up front with me about it, at least. I guess my last question is, when do I start?"

"As far as I'm concerned," said Foley, extending his hand, "you already have."

"So it looks like I finally figured out a way to make some money off my powers," said Henry. He had just wrapped up a truncated account of his encounter with Foley and Tyker as he and his family ate their green bean casserole dinner. "Isn't that awesome? This'll change everything!"

"Yeah, not too bad," said his dad with a chuckle, "as long as you don't just take off with the money and forget about your dear old parents,"

"Oh, come on," said Henry. "You know I won't do that until at *least* a couple weeks from now."

"I don't like this," said Henry's mother. "Who are these

guys? And why do they want to employ a teenage boy? Are they perverts or something?"

"I don't know, mom. I'll ask them," said Henry. "But in the meantime, I'll have to assume that even if they are perverts, they're not stupid enough to try anything with a guy who can lift a car over his head. So don't worry. Besides, I'm not just any teenage boy here."

"Well, it's not just that," his mother said. "This sounds like a very dangerous job. I don't want you going out there and getting hurt. I have half a mind to call these men up myself and ask them what it is exactly that they think they're doing, putting a young boy in harm's way. It's just not right."

"I'll be fine, mom! Trust me," said Henry through a mouthful of casserole. "I can handle myself. I just saved the entire town twice in a row all by my lonesome, didn't I? At least with these guys I'll have a ton of help. I'll barely need to do anything at all. And I'll be using my abilities to help people, to save lives, which is pretty noble, I think."

"Yes, but let's not forget that you just got out of the

hospital, Henry," said his mother.

"Then let's also not forget that these guys I'm working with are getting the cost of all my medical bills covered too. This is a good thing, trust me. Right, grandma?"

Henry's grandmother, who had been silent throughout the meal, looked over at him with baleful eyes. She blinked and picked at her food. "Whatever you say, dear," she said softly. "You seem to be able to take care of yourself."

"Mother!" said Henry's mom. "You can't be serious. With all the worrying you do about Henry, you would actually condone this?"

"It's too late anyway," Henry's grandmother said. She avoided everyone's eyes as she looked about the table.

"What do you-" said Henry's mother. She was cut off by a brief loop of extremely irritating music.

"Oop, my phone," said Henry. He pulled it out of his pocket and answered it. "Hello?"

"How many times have I told you not to talk on the phone at the dinner table?" said Henry's mother, fruitlessly.

"Can you believe this? We're actually going to have some money!" said Henry's father.

"I can't believe *you*. You're going along with this?"

Henry's father shrugged. "I like eating. And it sounds kind of cool. Maybe I should see if they'll hire me, too."

Henry hung his phone up. "Sorry, my friends are outside, so I've gotta go. I'll see you guys later."

"But-" said Henry's mother.

"Doesn't anybody knock on the door anymore? It's always phone calls now," said his father.

"Have a good night, guys! Love ya!" said Henry. As he left, he slammed the door with a bit too much enthusiasm. The wood splintered at the hinges and as Henry headed down the walkway toward Doug's waiting vehicle, the front door creaked, teetered backwards, and slammed to the floor.

Henry's father sighed. "Guess I'll go see if the hardware store's still open."

"So how're you feeling, man?" said Doug as Henry lowered himself into the passenger seat of the car. "You were in pretty rough shape last time I saw you."

"Not bad," said Henry. "I'll tell you this: I'd rather get my ribs busted again than have to sit through another interrogation by Sheriff Porter. Lord have mercy."

In the back seat, Trent guffawed. "You don't say! Guy always seemed like such a barrel of laughs to me."

Henry groaned. "God! I'll never smash up a cop car again!"

"Oh, you always say that," said Doug with a smirk. "So…are we karaokeing it?"

"Only if your irresponsible ass stays sober," said Trent.

"Hey, pot?" Doug shouted back. "Kettle. Black."

"Yeah. Let's go. Let's just be a little less crazy this time," said Henry.

"That's for sure. My toilet and I are in agreement that we don't want a repeat of your going away party," said Doug.

"And here I didn't even have the courtesy to go away afterwards." Henry whirled around in his seat and faced Albert. "So everything's good? You and Jenny doing OK?"

"Yeah," said Albert. "She was a little ticked at me at first because she thought I had abandoned her when the dance got...you know, out of hand. But I explained everything and I think it's smoothed over. She's actually supposed to meet up with us tonight."

"Great. *Another* female in this group. Like we don't have enough already," said Trent.

"I sincerely hope you're not talking about me," said Albert. "What about you, Henry? Talked to Denise?"

"A little. I don't know," Henry said. "I guess I have a lot to catch you guys up on, though. Good thing we have all night."

"Well, if you have anything important to say, better do it now before Trent ruptures our eardrums with that audio assault he calls singing," said Doug.

"Like you're any better," said Trent.

"Seriously," said Henry, "I'm just happy to see you guys. I'm glad you're all doing well, and we're going to have fun tonight. I just feel really fortunate to have you guys in my life, is all."

Trent made a gagging noise. Doug laughed and said, "Here we go. Getting all sentimental, are we? I think I liked you better when you were acting like a jerk. Now I'm just uncomfortable."

"Oh, shut up," said Henry. He looked out the window as the boys zoomed past rows of small homes, with their leaf-covered yards and winking porch lights. The town was quiet, save the wind's gentle whisper and the chugging of the car's motor. Henry felt every breath in his chest against his still-sore ribs, and lay back in his seat, temporarily tuned-out to the frivolous conversation around him. He was overwhelmed with joy at having a moment to just relax, to enjoy the company of his friends, to let go of the anxiety of being under the gun, of being sand in someone else's hourglass. Yet he was haunted by the feeling that a chapter of his life had just ended, that things were irrevocably changed in some way. A sense of uncertainty about what lay ahead had crept into his thoughts, the scale of which was uncomfortably foreign. Henry turned from the window and rejoined the conversation, which had somehow become about the incident with the urine-soaked P.E. uniform.

"Guys, I really thought we were past this," he said.

As the boys laughed, the car turned down a narrow street toward the part of downtown that had escaped destruction. With the waning moon an oversized Cheshire grin in the sky, surrounded by a shimmering sea of stars, the car sped into the darkness, a vehicle commanded by four young men in search of whatever strange adventures the fates had in store for them. For that night at least, the world was theirs.